# Lori Foster
# MR. NOVEMBER

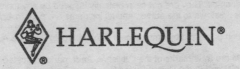

HARLEQUIN®

TORONTO • NEW YORK • LONDON
AMSTERDAM • PARIS • SYDNEY • HAMBURG
STOCKHOLM • ATHENS • TOKYO • MILAN • MADRID
PRAGUE • WARSAW • BUDAPEST • AUCKLAND

To Lt. Espinosa for incredible inspiration,
insight and research information.

Not only does he risk his life for the community, he went one further and organized a charity calendar to benefit others—and still found time to answer all my questions. I'm sure I'm not alone in my sincere gratitude to him for all he does.

*Here's to firefighters everywhere—*
*a truly heroic service. Our thanks!*

ISBN 0-373-25956-5

MR. NOVEMBER

Copyright © 2001 by Lori Foster.

# 1

## Josh

WITH GREAT INTEREST, Amanda Barker peeked into the locker room. She'd been at the fire station—*hounding him*—many times, but she'd never ventured into this private area.

There was a partitioned off shower area adjacent to the room, and steam from recent use still crept around the ceiling, leaving the air damp and thick. A few of the lockers stood open and empty. Discarded white towels littered the floor, the benches and an array of varnished wooden chairs. Amanda wrinkled her nose. The room smelled of men and smoke, soap and sweat.

Except for the smoke, it wasn't an unpleasant odor.

On the far wall, opposite the door she'd entered, a framed copy of the *Firefighter's Prayer* hung slightly askew, droplets of water beading on the glass cover. Next to that, a plaque reading Always Loved, Never Forgotten, listed local firefighters who had died in community service.

Amanda drew a shaky breath and crept inside. The

prayer drew her and she found herself standing in front of it, reading words she already knew by heart.

*Enable me to be alert, and hear the weakest shout, and quickly and efficiently to put the fire out.* She touched the glass covering those incredible words, wiping away the moisture. She dropped her hand and turned away, troubled as always whenever she remembered.

With self-taught discipline, she shook off the familiar feelings and surveyed her surroundings.

The locker room and connecting showers appeared empty, but she knew he was in there. The watchman had told her so—had even given her permission to go in, smiling all the while, ready to conspire with her to get their most infamous lieutenant to finally cooperate.

Behind her in the main rooms, she heard firefighters talking, laughing as the new shift arrived and the others headed home. They were a flirtatious lot, sometimes crude, always macho and fun loving to counteract the heavy responsibilities of their jobs. They were also in prime condition, lean and hard, thanks to rigorous physical training.

They all looked good, and they all knew it. With only one exception, they were willing—even eager— to help her out with the charity calendar by posing for various months. The money they made selling the calendar would benefit the local burn institute.

Amanda hoped none of the men came in behind her; it was past time she and Josh Marshall got things settled. Since the start of the project he'd refused to take part and avoided her whenever she tried to convince him. He even failed to return her calls.

The man was bullheaded and selfish and she intended to tell him so, but she didn't want an audience. Confrontations were not her thing. In fact, she avoided them whenever possible.

*He* wouldn't let her avoid this one.

Much as she hated to admit it, she needed Josh Marshall. She needed him to understand the importance of what she hoped to do, and then she needed his agreement to take part in her newest charity effort. While it was true all the men looked good, Josh Marshall looked better than good. He looked great. Sexy. Hot. He'd make the perfect Mr. November and the perfect model for the cover. They'd use him in advertising in local papers, bookstores and on the Web.

One way or another, Amanda intended to get his agreement today.

A muted sound, like the padding of bare feet on wet concrete, reached her ears. She turned and there he stood, all six-feet-plus of him. Casual as you please, a man without a care, he leaned in the doorframe. His blond hair was wet, his muscles were wet and the skimpy towel barely hooked around his lean hips was wet.

Slow rivulets of water dripped over his chest and through his body hair, slinking down his ridged abdomen and into the towel. He had his arms and ankles crossed. The towel parted, and one bare hairy thigh was exposed all the way to the lighter skin of his hip, up to the insubstantial knot in the towel. It wouldn't take much more than a very tiny tug to remove that towel.

She'd seen him in his lieutenant's uniform, she'd seen him hot and sweaty fresh from a fire, and she'd seen him relaxed, sitting around the station, on duty but not occupied.

She'd never seen him mostly naked and it was definitely...an eye-opener.

Amanda stood a little straighter and met his gaze. She had to tip her head back because he stood so much taller than she did. At only five feet four inches, she was used to that and refused to let it bother her now, just because the man was mostly naked and *trying* to bother her. She said, "Lieutenant Marshall."

His dark green eyes, so often remote in her presence, now looked her over, starting at her dress pumps and advancing to her soft pink suit and up to the small pearl studs in her ears. He gave a crooked smile and sauntered three steps to a locker. "Ms. Barker." He opened the locker and pulled out a bottle of cologne, splashing a bit in his hands, then patting his face and throat.

His scent overrode that of the smoke, and Amanda breathed him in, all warm damp skin, clean soap and that dark, earthy scent he'd just added. She recognized it from previous contact, but now was different. Now his big body was mostly bare.

Her nostrils quivered and she took an involuntary step back, bumping into the wall.

Of course, he noticed; his smile told her so, the glitter in his dark green eyes told her so. She held her breath, waiting to see what he'd say, how he'd mock her, and instead he reached for a comb. He turned to face her fully while tidying his hair. "How'd you get in here, anyway?"

Never in her life had she watched a man groom himself. Josh Marshall...well, it was unexpected. The heavy muscles in his raised arms flexed and bulged as he dragged the black comb straight back through his wet hair. She could see his underarms and the soft, darker hair there. Her heart bumped into her ribs with startling force. Somehow, that part of Josh seemed more intimate than his exposed thighs and abdomen.

"Cat got your tongue?" He reached for a T-shirt, which he pulled on over his head with casual disregard for the hair he'd just combed. The front of the shirt read: Firefighters Find 'Em Hot—and Leave 'Em Wet.

Her pulse raced and she had to clear her throat before she could speak coherently. "The watchman let me in so we could talk."

"You're a persistent little thing, aren't you?"

She ignored the sexist comment even as she acknowledged it for truth; she was persistent, and she was most certainly little. "You haven't returned any of my calls."

"No, I haven't, have I?" His deep voice held only mild interest in her visit. "Ever wonder why?"

As he asked that, he lifted out a pair of black cotton boxers and she just barely had time to avert her face before he pulled the towel away.

Cheeks scalding, Amanda gave him her back. "You're being stubborn."

"Actually, I was trying to be direct. I don't want to do the calendar, so there's no point in wasting my time or yours."

"But I need you."

Amanda felt the pause, his utter stillness in response to her words, and wanted to bite off her own tongue. Instead, she asked impatiently, "Are you decent?"

He gave a short laugh. "Never."

"I meant..." She wanted to groan, she wanted to ask him why he had to taunt her and be so impossible. But that wouldn't win him over so she drew a breath and asked instead, "Have you got your pants on?"

"Yeah."

She turned, and saw he'd only been half-truthful. He wore his boxers and the T-shirt, but that was all. Even sitting on the bench, his jeans next to him, he looked more manly than any man she knew. His large hands were braced on the bleached wood of the bench at either side of his hips, his powerful thighs casually sprawled, his gaze direct.

Amanda could see the bulge of his sex in his underwear and found herself staring. It was a contrast, the sight of that soft, cuddled weight when the rest of him was so hard and lean.

"Should I take them back off?"

She jerked her gaze to his face and asked stupidly, "What?"

"The underwear." His voice was silky, the words and meaning hot. "I can skin them off if you wanna get a better look."

She started to laugh to cover her embarrassment over being caught, except that he looked serious. Was he enough of a reprobate to do as he suggested? One look into those intense green eyes and she knew the answer was an unequivocal *yes*.

In fact, he looked...anxious to do so.

She'd allowed things to get way out of hand. "Lieutenant—"

"Why don't you call me Josh? Being as you just stroked me with those pretty brown eyes, I feel we're on more personal terms now."

"No." Amanda shook her head. "I apologize for the staring. It was dreadful of me, I admit it, and I promise you it won't happen again. But I prefer to keep things professional."

"Oh, but that won't do." Josh stood and that damn crooked smile warned her that she wouldn't like what was about to come next.

She edged to the side, ready to escape him, and banged into an open locker. Her high heels threw her off balance and she nearly fell before catching herself.

Josh didn't give her time to be embarrassed over her lack of grace. He stalked her, his gaze locked onto hers as he closed in, refusing to let her look away.

He came right up to her and crowded her back until the only air she could breathe was heated and scented by his big body, until the only thing she could see was his broad hard chest in that dark T-shirt.

Flattening his hands on the locker at either side of her head, he caged her in. His thick wrists, incredibly hot, touched her temples.

*"Lieutenant..."* Amanda seldom panicked anymore; the feelings had been tempered by seven years of distance. But at the moment, panic seemed her wisest choice.

"Uh-uh," he murmured, "none of that." Very slowly, suggestively, he leaned down, making her think he might kiss her and bringing her very close to a scream.

She froze, her heartbeat skipping, her pulse racing. One second, two... The kiss never came and a riot of emotions bombarded her, none of them easily distinguishable except relief and a faint feeling of disappointment. He made a small sound of surprise, as if she'd somehow taken him off guard, and her damn knees went weak.

His nose touched her neck and he inhaled deeply.

Amanda quivered. *"What* are you doing?"

"I've decided how I'm going to handle you, Amanda." His hot breath brushed her ear, sending gooseflesh up and down her spine. She was aware of the cool contrast of his damp hair grazing her cheek.

*Handle her?* She couldn't move a single inch without touching him somewhere. She held very still. "What are you talking about?"

He tilted his head away to smile into her shocked face. Watching her with heavy eyes and a load of expectation, he said, "I want you in my bed."

Her mouth fell open.

No, surely he hadn't just said... But he had! He'd actually suggested... Amanda laughed. Such a ridiculous, ludicrous...

Shaking her head, she managed to say, "No, you really don't."

He looked a little confounded by her reaction. He tilted his head and narrowed his eyes to study her. "Now there's where you're wrong, sweetheart. You've been pursuing me—"

"For a charity event!"

"—for over a month now. I decided it was time I did the pursuing. And once I thought of it, I couldn't think of anything else." His gaze wandered over her face, and landed on her mouth. He leaned in again. "Damn, you smell good."

Of all the bizarre things that could have happened, Amanda hadn't expected this one. Josh Marshall coming on to her? A man who wouldn't normally look at her without frowning, a man who only told her 'no,' when he bothered to tell her anything at all?

Her reserve melted away, replaced by the unshakable facade of apathy she'd built years ago. Josh Marshall didn't matter to her, so he couldn't hurt her. No one could.

Her heart now safely concealed, her mind clear, she put both hands on Josh's chest to lever him back.

He allowed her the small distance.

Hoping she sounded reasonable, she said, "Lieutenant, you can trust me on this one, okay? You don't want me. You're not in the least interested in me."

"I didn't think so at first, either." His hands covered hers, keeping them snug against his chest. Under the circumstances, she barely registered the firm muscles, the heat of his skin through the soft cotton and the relaxed thumping of his heart. "But as I said, I've changed my mind."

Gently, because she hoped to nip his outlandish plan in the bud without causing any hard feelings between them, she said, "Then unchange it, Lieutenant. Really."

He looked a little baffled by her response to his come-on. She nearly smirked. No doubt most women would have been simpering, eager to get to know him better, excited by the prospect of sharing his bed.

Amanda shuddered. She didn't waste her time on impossible dreams, and she definitely didn't waste it on men. Not in that way.

The reasons behind her behavior didn't matter. What mattered was that Josh Marshall not pursue her. That scenario would only agitate them both.

He lifted a hand to her cheek and gently stroked

with his fingertips. His gaze appeared troubled, concerned and sympathetic. In a voice barely above a whisper, he asked, "What are you so afraid of?"

Amanda almost fell over. Her throat closed and her knees stiffened. No! He couldn't possibly see her fear. She kept it well hidden and buried so deep, no one, not even her family, ever saw it. Men accused her of being frigid, gay, a total bitch...but none of them ever noticed the gnawing fear she lived with.

"Shh. It's all right. I just didn't know." Josh continued to touch her, and then he stepped away. Not far, but at least she could breathe. He stared into her widened eyes and said with a mix of gentleness and determination, "Whatever it is, Amanda, we'll go slow. I promise."

"We won't go at all!" Her heart thumped so hard it hurt and her stomach felt queasy. She pressed a fist to her belly and sought lost composure. "I'm not in the least interested, Josh... Lieutenant Marshall."

He smiled. "Oh, you're interested. I wager you've even considered things between us a time or two. Maybe a hot fantasy late at night?"

"You'd be pathetically wrong." The bite in her words was unavoidable; she did not, ever, delude herself with fantasies.

Taken aback by her vehemence, Josh whistled low. "An abusive ex? Poor home life?"

"No and no."

Rubbing his chin, he said, "You might as well tell me. I'll get it out of you sooner or later."

The man was impossible! "Why do you even want to?"

He shrugged. "It's obvious there's a problem, and we can't get on to the lovemaking until it's solved."

Her mouth fell open again. "My God, your conceit is incredible."

"Confidence, not conceit." He lifted one massive shoulder. "I know women, inside and out. You're hiding something, something that scares the hell out of you, and now I'm doubly intrigued. All in all, I'm beginning to think this is going to be fun. Not at all the chore I'd first envisioned."

His every word, every action, threw her. She caught herself barking a very unladylike laugh. "A chore? *A chore.* You expect to ingratiate yourself with me using comments like that?"

He winked as he pulled on his jeans and sat on the bench again to don socks and lace up black boots. "I don't want to win you over, sweetheart. I just want you in my bed."

Tension prickled her nerve endings, started the low thrum of a headache. Amanda rubbed her temples, trying to think. "We've gotten off course here somehow." She drew a steadying breath and dredged up a vague smile. "All I want is for you to agree to have your picture taken. An hour of your time..."

Josh stood and began threading a thick black leather belt through his belt loops. "Have dinner with me."

An audible click sounded when her teeth snapped together. "No. Thank you."

He buckled the belt and pulled out a black leather jacket, slinging it over his shoulder and hooking it with his thumb. He looked her over, the epitome of male arrogance and savage resolve. "I thought we'd discuss the calendar."

Indecision warred with hope. Would he relent and allow her to get the photographs she needed? Was he just leading her on to get his way?

The biggest question was whether or not she could handle him—and she had serious doubts on that issue. In a thousand different ways, she knew Josh Marshall was unlike any other man she'd encountered. He was persuasive, a lady's man in every sense of the word, walking testosterone with an abundance of charm. To top it off, he had a killer body that got double takes from females of all ages.

They *wouldn't* end up in bed, of course, so that wasn't a real worry for Amanda. His confidence and past successes were irrelevant. The worry was how much hell he'd put her through before he accepted defeat. Somehow, she didn't think he took defeat very well.

In her case, he'd have to learn.

But if he would agree to the calendar, did it really matter if she had to put up with his seduction tactics first? She would resist because she had to, and in the end, she'd get what *she* wanted.

With a sense of dread, in spite of the pep talk that

she'd just given herself, Amanda nodded. "All right."

Josh's expression softened. "I promise it won't be near the degradation you're imagining."

"Not at all." She needed his agreement, and antagonizing him would gain her nothing but his continued refusal. "The dinner will be fine, I'm sure."

Without her permission, he walked up to her and put his large muscled arm around her back. She felt the heat of his hand as it opened on her waist. Before she could react, he urged her forward.

"I have a few rules we can discuss on the way out."

"Rules?" She felt vague and uncertain with him touching her so much.

"That's right. And rule number one is that you have to call me Josh. No more 'Lieutenant' formality."

She could live with that. "If you insist."

"Rule two—no discussions of any actual fires. I like to leave my job behind when I'm off duty."

"Agreed." Amanda realized she'd answered a tad too quickly when Josh stopped and looked down at her. The last thing she wanted to discuss, now or ever, was a real fire. "I...I understand," she stammered, trying to keep him from looking inside her again.

For a long moment, he just stood there, considering her, and then he nodded. "Let's go."

As they walked through the station, firemen looked up. A few laughed, a few called out suggestions and Josh, without slowing, made a crude gesture in their general direction and kept going. But when Amanda peeked up at his face, she saw his satisfied...maybe smug, smile.

Ha! Let him be smug, she didn't care. All she cared about was her project.

And that meant she had to care about him. But just for a little while.

JOSH WATCHED Amanda as they stepped outside into the cool October night. He was just coming off a twelve-hour shift, and after two emergency calls that day, he should have been tired. He *had* been tired, clear down to the bone. He'd thought only of getting home and falling into bed. But now he was... expectant. And a little horny.

*For Amanda Barker.* He grinned.

There'd been a recent drizzle and the station's lights, as well as a bright moon, glistened across the wet pavement. The cool air was brisk, stirred by an uneasy breeze.

It matched his mood.

With his hand on Amanda's back, he could feel the nervousness she tried so hard to hide. It wasn't a reaction he was used to from women. But then Amanda wasn't what he was used to.

She also wasn't what he wanted, not even close.

Not that it seemed to matter tonight.

Once he'd made up his mind to turn the tables on her, he'd found himself thinking about her a lot.

About getting her out of her perfect little feminine suits and letting down her perfectly coiffed hair.

He wanted to see if Amanda Barker could stop being so sweet and refined and classy. He wanted to see her wild, unreserved.

He wanted to hear her screaming out a climax, to feel her perfectly painted pink nails digging into his back as she bucked beneath him.

Josh stopped and drew a deep breath. He put his hands on his hips and dropped his head forward with a laugh. Damn, he'd let his lust get out of hand.

He hadn't expected her here tonight, had in fact been too wiped out from the emergency calls to do much thinking at all. Yet, she'd surprised him by hanging out in the locker room, waiting for *him*.

A pleasant surprise and a very nice distraction.

He'd made his decision a week ago and had been thinking about it ever since. At least a dozen different ways, he'd imagined their encounter, how he'd approach her and what he'd say, how she'd react to his come-on.

Not once had he imagined seeing fear on her face.

"Lieutenant Marshall?"

He whipped his head up and snared her gaze, making her brown eyes widen in startled reaction. "Josh, remember?"

"Sorry." She licked her bottom lip, apparently undecided, then that iron determination of hers came to the fore and she stiffened like a sail caught in the wind. "Josh, is something wrong? Because I want you to know if you've changed your mind—about dinner I mean—that's fine with me. We can just set up a time for the shoot and part ways here."

She really, truly, wanted nothing to do with him.

Josh hated being forced to face his own ego, but...he was stunned. Oh, he'd known women who hadn't wanted to be involved with him. He was twenty-seven years old and he'd had his fair share of rejections. Women who were already involved or those who didn't like the risks associated with his work. Women who'd been looking for marriage and those who'd just gotten divorced and needed time to regroup.

Most recently, he'd been rebuffed by two incredible women who'd chosen his best friends instead. He smiled at that, thinking how happy Mick and Zack were.

Oh, Wynn and Delilah liked him, they even doted on him occasionally, but only as a friend.

Other than Amanda, he'd never suffered complete and total disinterest.

*Why* she was so disinterested was something he intended to find out.

"I haven't changed my mind." Josh saw her delicate jaw tighten and felt just perverse enough to add, "I was imagining how you might be in bed. If you'd be so prissy and ladylike then, or if you'd really let go. Maybe do a little screaming or something."

A variety of expressions crossed her face in rapid succession—mortification, incredulity and finally, fury. She turned away from him, her arms crossed under her breasts.

The first words she spoke took him by surprise. "I'm *not* prissy."

A slow grin started and spread until he almost laughed out loud. Had he managed to prick her vanity? "No?" He drawled the question, just to infuriate her more. "Seem prissy to me. I can't know for sure, but I'm willing to bet even your toenails are painted, aren't they?"

"So?"

He'd love to see her feet. They were small and narrow and forever arched in sexy high heels. She had great calves, but the skirts she wore were too long to see her thighs, more's the pity.

"It's cold." She stared up at the glowing moon, rubbed her arms briskly and shivered. "Do you mean to stand here and insult me all night?"

Amanda had pulled on a soft, cream-colored cashmere coat with matching leather gloves. The outerwear was fashionable, but probably not very warm.

He could warm her, but she didn't look receptive to that idea. "I didn't consider it an insult. More like an observation."

"Then I'd hate to hear your idea of an insult."

Even miffed, she looked picture-perfect...and about as approachable as a china doll.

The woman stymied him. But then, he was up for a challenge.

Holding out his hand to her, Josh said, "My car's this way."

She slanted a suspicious, sideways glance at him. "Just tell me where we're going and I'll meet you there."

Hell, no. Now that he had her, he wouldn't take any chances on her changing her mind. For some reason, being with her tonight mattered more with each passing second. "Nope. We ride together."

Her face fell. "But I have my car with me." She gestured toward the street to a powder blue Volkswagen Beetle. Not the new spiffy version, but an older model.

Josh did a double take. That car most definitely did not fit her image of refined ladylike grace. The car looked...playful.

Amanda Barker was chock full of secrets. First, that disbelieving laugh when he'd propositioned her. Then her indignation at the suggestion she might be prissy, which was a bona fide fact as far as Josh was concerned. And now that fun car. He shook his head.

He could discuss the car with her later, Josh decided. "So? I'll bring you back here for it after dinner." She looked ready to refuse, and he added, "We can discuss the calendar along the way."

That easily, she gave in. "Very well." She stepped closer, but stayed just out of reach of his extended hand.

Challenged, Josh snagged her arm and held on to

it. She didn't pull away, but her nose did go into the air.

She had a beautiful profile, especially with her features softened by the shadows of the night and the opalescent sheen of the moon. Her neck was even graceful, and looked very kissable with tiny tendrils of tawny hair teasing her nape.

"Do you always wear your hair up?" He tried to imagine it loose, to guess how long or thick it might be.

In a voice snooty enough for a queen, she said, "My hair has nothing to do with dinner or the calendar."

"It has to do with my fantasies though." He tightened his hold when he felt her preparing to slip away. He lowered his voice and said, "I close my eyes at night and imagine your hair hanging free. Sometimes I can almost feel it on my stomach, or my thighs."

She stopped so abruptly he nearly pulled her off her high heels. Gathering her poise and clutching her purse in front of her like a blockade, she said, "This is sexual harassment!"

Actually, it had turned into a wet dream a few nights ago, but Josh thought it might not be a good time to share that with her. "I see you're out of practice."

Indecision and frustration tightened her features. "What do you mean?"

Leaning close, Josh touched the end of her reddening nose and said, "Seduction, sweetheart. Not harassment."

"I don't *want* to be seduced!"

A couple of passersby stared, then laughed before hurrying away.

Josh took her arm and started her on her way again. "Take deep breaths, Amanda. It'll be okay."

One gloved hand covered her mouth. "Oh God, this is just awful."

He didn't want to say it, but he couldn't let her start thinking of his pursuit as harassment. "You don't have to be here, you know. You don't work for me, I have no hold over you—"

"I need you for the calendar!"

"No," he said, giving her arm a gentle squeeze, "you *want* me for the calendar."

Miffed, she grouched, "I don't know why. You're absolutely—"

"Sticks and stones may break my bones..."

She looked like she wanted to scream again, but instead she stopped and straightened her shoulders, her spine. She pasted on a serene expression and even managed a smile.

*Poor little thing*, he thought. She worked so hard at maintaining all that elegant dignity when what she really wanted to do, what her nature demanded she do, was turn loose her temper and wallop him. He waited, anxious to hear what she'd say.

With shaking fingers she tidied her already tidy hair and smoothed her coat. "Where will we be eating?"

Josh waggled a finger at her. "That was way too restrained. I had myself all prepared and then, nothing but fizzle. I'd say I'm disappointed, but I think that's what you're after." He leaned down to his car, unlocked and opened the door. "In you go."

"This is yours?"

"Yep. Like it?"

She admired the shiny black Firebird convertible. "It's very nice. Very...macho." She settled herself inside, placing her feet just so, her hands in her lap. Amused, Josh reached around her to hook her seat belt.

"Oh!" She pressed herself back in the seat, avoiding any contact with him. "I can do that."

"I've got it." He liked buckling her in, taking care of her. He smoothed the belt into place, and in the process, skimmed her stomach with the backs of his fingers. Even through her clothes and a winter coat, the simple touch aroused him.

Pathetic.

He'd have laughed at himself, but he was too busy inhaling her perfume. He'd first caught the soft, seductive scent in the locker room, and it had been all he could do not to kiss her. With his nearness, her shiny pink-painted lips had trembled, enticing him.

But the panicked look in her deep brown eyes—a look she didn't want him to see—had struck him deep.

Someone had hurt her, and he didn't like it.

Josh walked around to the driver's side, using the moment to come to grips with himself. Amanda wasn't a woman he should involve himself with. She appealed to him sexually, but she wasn't his normal type, wasn't the type of woman he'd come to appreciate.

She wasn't at all like Delilah or Wynonna. They were casual women, up front and honest and outspoken. He'd learned to appreciate those qualities.

Amanda, on the other hand, was so buttoned up she might as well have been wearing armor. And secrets! He was beginning to think everything about her was a mystery.

He'd meant to tease her, maybe teach her a lesson by turning the tables on her. He'd definitely meant to make love to her. Probably more than once.

But he hadn't meant to start delving into her past, discovering her ghosts, involving himself in her life.

Yet, he knew it was too late. Like it or not, he was already involved. And it hadn't taken any work on her part to get him there. No, she wanted nothing to do with him beyond using him for her damned calendar.

Josh intended to change all that.

But first there was something he had to know. As soon as he pulled into traffic, he girded himself, took a deep breath, and asked as casually as he could manage, "Are you afraid of me, Amanda?"

## 2

"WHAT?" AMANDA'S confused frown was genuine, relieving Josh on that score.

He shrugged. "We both know you're afraid of something. I just wanted to make sure it wasn't me."

She went rigid with indignation. "You do not frighten me, Lieutenant."

"Ah, ah," Josh chastised. He reached over and tickled her chin before she jerked away. "There you go again with that Lieutenant stuff. It's Josh. We have an agreement."

Silence fell heavily in the car, then she sighed. "Where are we going for dinner?"

He wasn't about to tell her, not yet. "Someplace nice and quiet, so we can talk. But nothing fancy."

"I'm not dressed for fancy anyway."

He glanced at her. Other than the lights of passing vehicles and streetlamps occasionally flickering by they were held in a cocoon of darkness. Her nose was narrow and straight and aristocratic. With her wide eyes, that stubborn chin and the most luscious mouth he'd ever fantasized over, she was a beauty.

But that wasn't what drew him. That wasn't what had him suddenly hot with need. He'd known plenty of women, beautiful and otherwise. No, it was something else, something he couldn't put his finger on yet.

"Amanda, you could go anywhere, anytime, and be suitably dressed." As far as compliments went, it was subtle, not in the least aggressive, nothing for her to shy away from.

But she didn't respond, so he added, "You always look great."

She ducked her head, then bit her bottom lip. "Thank you." She quickly added, "Now, about the calendar. I'd like to discuss something special for your photo."

"Special?" He wasn't at all sure he liked the sound of that. In fact, the very idea of the calendar bugged him. Firefighters should, in his mind, be respected for the hard work they did, not just for their bodies. The whole beefcake approach didn't sit well with him.

"That's right. I want to put you on the cover and use you for the promotions."

If he hadn't been driving, he'd have closed his eyes with disgust. The cover. Damn.

With the new topic, Amanda had turned all businesslike on him, twisting in her seat to face him, her expression more animated, open. Because Josh liked the change and enjoyed seeing her less reserved, he didn't immediately disregard her offer.

"Why?"

She blinked at him. "Why what?"

"Why do you want to use me for the cover?"

Confusion showed on her beautiful face, then chagrin. She gestured at him, her small, gloved hand flapping the air. "Well...look at you, for heaven's sake. Out of all the firemen who agreed to take part, you're by far the most handsome, and you have a fabulous physique."

"You noticed, huh?"

Amanda rolled her eyes. "Because those assets will certainly help sell calendars—which is the whole point—yes I noticed. You're the obvious choice."

Josh drove in silence for a moment, his hands relaxed on the wheel, his thoughts hidden. Only the hissing of tires on wet pavement intruded. That, and her scent.

Her scent was making him nuts.

"I've got a question for you." He pulled into the parking lot of a take-out chicken joint. It didn't look like much, but he knew firsthand how good the food was.

Amanda looked around in consternation. "We're eating here?"

Josh ignored her question to ask one of his own. "If you think I look so good, why in hell do you refuse to get involved with me?" He pulled in to the line for the drive-thru. There were two cars ahead of him, so he braked and turned to face her.

She had her purse clutched tightly in her lap and that panicked look on her face again. "What are you doing?"

Because he knew she'd already figured it out, he said gently, "I'm buying some food."

Her chest rose and fell with agitated breaths. "For what?" She looked ready to leap from his car.

Josh reached across the seat and touched her cheek. His heart squeezed tight when she leaned away from him and that awesome fear widened her eyes and drained the color from her face.

His plan had gone horribly awry, he thought. He didn't want to tease her, didn't want to taunt her.

He just wanted her—sexually, and otherwise.

"For us to eat," he admitted, watching her closely, trying to better read her. "At my place—where as I said, it's nice and quiet and we can talk."

It was the last that got her. She jerked around, blindly, wildly reaching for the door handle. She yanked on it, but the door was locked.

"Amanda..."

She made a small sound, incoherent except for that damn fear.

Josh didn't know what the hell to do. Never in his blighted life had he dealt with a hysterical woman— hysterical because she didn't want to be with him!

Luckily, her seat belt restrained her so he didn't have to chase her through the parking lot.

Josh kept his tone calm and soothing. "What are you doing? I can take you back to your car if you don't want to have dinner after all. You don't have to walk." He sounded like an ass and hated himself. But she listened. "It's just that... I'm exhausted after two emergency calls on one shift. I want to relax, not sit in a public place."

That sounded plausible to him. Pleased with his excuse—entirely made up—he waited.

Amanda paused, facing the window, her shoulders hunched. In a small voice, she said, "I don't see why we need to go to your place."

"We don't." Minutes ago, he'd have tried insisting, now he just wanted her to relax again. "Hell, we can eat here if you want. Or in the parking lot."

She looked at him over her shoulder. "You're really that tired?"

Enormous relief washed over him. "Yeah." He smiled. "You should have seen me in the shower."

Her eyes widened and he laughed. "Get those lecherous thoughts out of your mind, woman. I meant because I was so tired, I sat on a chair to shower. All of us did."

She shifted around, interested, calmer. The line moved at the same time, and Josh drove forward.

"Why?" she asked.

"I told you, exhaustion. We keep these old wooden chairs in the shower for such occasions." She looked fascinated, and he found himself breaking one of his rules. "After a fire, it's often like that. The adrenaline fades and you're left weary down to the bone, filthy with grime and soot."

His heart jumped when he felt Amanda touch his arm.

"I'm sorry."

He practically held his breath. Women touched him all the time, damn it, and in more interesting places than his elbow. But her touch...it meant something. And he liked it. "For what?"

"For acting so foolish. It's just that sometimes..."

Josh reached for her hand, laced his fingers with hers. When she didn't pull away, he felt as if the sun had just come out and shone on his miserable head. "Sometimes you get afraid? You remember something and you find yourself just reacting?"

She stared at their entwined hands. "Josh, I want to be honest with you, okay?"

He waited.

She transferred his hand to both of hers. "I meant what I said." Her gaze was direct, unflinching. "I know lots of women adore you. I even understand why. But I really, truly, am not interested. I don't want you to understand me, I don't need your friendship or your affection. Of course I have...issues. Everyone does. But I like my life the way it is and I have no intention of changing a single thing." Her gaze implored his understanding. "All I need, all I want, is for you to agree to pose for the calendar."

Josh rested back in his seat and studied her. Whatever plagued her, he wouldn't find out about it tonight. Tactics that usually had women laughing and flirting back only fell flat with her. He needed a new plan, and he needed it now.

He made a sudden decision. "I'll do the pose."

She released him to clasp her hands together in excitement. Her face lit up. "You will?"

It was his turn at the drive-thru and he gave her a long look before pulling up to the order window. Despite everything she'd just said, he ordered enough for two.

After the food was handed to them and safely stored on the floorboards, Josh clarified. "I'll do the calendar, but I won't stop wanting you. And I won't stop trying to change your mind about wanting me."

He heard her gasp, but damn it, she couldn't expect him to just walk away. Not now.

As he eased back into traffic, he stared out the windshield into the endless black night. "It's your decision Amanda. If you have me in the calendar, then you'll have to deal with my courtship."

"Courtship, ha!"

Josh hid his smile. At least now she wasn't squashed up against the opposite door, doing her best to put a mile between them. She was facing him, talking to him, and he chose to see that as progress. "Make up your mind, okay? You can either walk away now and use one of the other guys to fill up the calendar, or you can learn to deal with me. And understand, sweetheart, I would never force you, and I'd never hurt you." He took the turn off the main drag to the quieter, emptier street leading toward his place.

"But I am determined," he finished saying, "to have my own way."

PIGHEADED LOUT.

Amanda stewed, unsure what to say next. Not only had she made a complete and total fool of herself, behaving like a spooked child, but she hadn't accomplished a thing with her honest, up-front admission to him. If anything, she was in deeper now that she'd spilled her heart.

True, Josh had listened. She'd felt his undivided attention. But then he'd disregarded everything she'd said.

She'd been truthful and so had he and now they were at an impasse. Amanda eyed him in the dark confines of the car and knew what she'd have to do.

Still, she gave it one more try. "It won't do you any good, you know."

"What? To chase after you? Hey, just call me an optimist." He smiled, looking so handsome and teasing. "Besides, I'm thinking you might be worth the trouble."

"I'm not."

"No?" He sounded amused. "How come?"

"Because you'll only be wasting your time."

"You think you're that boring, do you?"

Tension tightened her fingers on the strap of her purse and made her neck ache. "Josh, I don't date and I don't do...anything else."

He turned speculative as he asked, "Anything else like kiss or fondle or make love?"

Closing her eyes only made her more aware of him beside her, a large hard man who exuded energy and heat. He threatened the foundation of her existence. Everything she'd worked so hard for, including emotional peace, had to be kept in the forefront of her mind. She could not let him distract her from her convictions.

She forced herself to look at him. "I can't imagine you'd be content to just share a chicken dinner with me every now and again."

His big hand patted her knee, startling her. "It's a start."

"It would also be the finish."

He retreated physically, but not verbally. "Again I have to ask, Amanda—how come?"

With no streetlights on the narrower road, the night was black and all she could see of Josh was a faint outline and the glitter of his eyes.

"That's none of your business." The fragrant smell of fried chicken teased her nostrils and Amanda's stomach rumbled. She was hungry, stressed and still hopeful. "Tonight we can iron out the details and tomorrow I'll bring a release form by the station. I'll leave it with the watchman. If you'd get it back to me right away, I'd appreciate it. We're really pressed for time—behind schedule actually."

"Because of me?" He turned down a cul-de-sac with duplex housing.

"I always try to do what's best for the project. I know you'll help sales, so yes, I held things up hoping you'd change your mind."

"Hoping you could change my mind."

"Yes. Everything's gone to the printers already, except the cover and the November photo, because those are what I'd like you to do. Once that's taken care of we can finish printing the first set of calendars and have them bound. They'll be ready for sale by early November, and we can cash in on some of the Christmas purchases."

Josh pulled into the driveway of a modern duplex home. He parked his car in an open garage spot, and with a remote, closed the garage door. "I'm to the left," he said, explaining which of the homes connected by the spacious two-car garage was his. He turned the headlights off and killed the engine, then turned to face Amanda.

Being in that closed garage made Amanda feel even more confined. Flustered, she started to open her car door, but Josh's long fingers closed around her upper arm. Panic, as fresh as it had been earlier, churned inside her.

What Josh didn't know, what he couldn't understand, was that her panic wasn't inspired by physical fear, but rather emotional. Her body didn't mind his touch at all, but her heart, her head, knew the danger in allowing him any familiarity at all. Seven years ago she had made a promise to herself, sworn to make reparations in the only way left to her, and she didn't want anything or anyone to sway her from that course.

She fought off the drowning emotions, drawing one breath, then two. She'd long ago learned that

they came from memories and overwhelming guilt—
she'd also learned to control them by isolating herself.

Josh wouldn't let her do that.

He caressed her arm. Through her outer coat, her
suit coat and her blouse, his touch was still disturbing. Amanda could detect the seductive strength in
his hand, the leashed tenderness that had likely lured
so many women.

Just as it lured her.

"Even this upsets you, doesn't it?"

The overhead garage light, which had come on
when he activated the door remote, now flickered off.
A blanket of inky darkness fell that was both a comfort for what it concealed, and a threat for what it un-
leashed. Her voice shook when she said, "I'd prefer
you quit touching me, yes."

She held her breath waiting for his reaction to that
statement, but all he said was, "Sit tight while I get
the light."

He left his car door open as he went to the door
leading into the house from the garage. Light spilled
out of the car and across the concrete floor, showing a
tidy display of tools. It also showed a heavy ax, hung
against a pegboard. For one brief moment Amanda
imagined Josh swinging that ax, ventilating a burning
house before the heat and smoke overtook him. She
gasped with the image, hurt and fearful.

The sudden bright light nearly blinded her. She
glanced up to see that Josh had unlocked the door

and reached inside for a wall switch. Now that she could see her way, Amanda opened her own door and climbed out. She took a single step and then Josh was there beside her—the consummate gentleman, the pushy contender, she wasn't sure which.

He reached into the car for the bucket of chicken and the bag of side dishes, then maintained his hold on her elbow as he led her inside.

They walked directly into an informal dining room. Josh plopped the food onto a thick cream-colored enamel table edged in shiny brass and surrounded by cream leather chairs. He reached for her coat and she had little choice but to slip it off. He put it over the back of a chair and while she removed her gloves, he shrugged out of his leather jacket.

All the while he watched her, leaving her unnerved and uncertain.

To escape his probing gaze, she looked around his home. The sparse dining room opened into a modern stainless steel kitchen and to the right of the kitchen was an archway leading into a living room. She could just see the edge of a beige leather couch with brass-and-glass end tables topped with colorful deco lamps. A short flight of carpeted stairs went up, likely to bedrooms, and a flight went down, maybe to a den.

He wasn't much for decorating, she noted. Most of the tabletops were barren; there were no photos or knickknacks about. Everything looked clean and utilitarian—perfect for a bachelor. She turned back to Josh with a smile. "Your home is lovely."

Hands on his hips, he asked, "So what's it to be? You wanna eat first and then talk, or talk first?"

"Eat."

The corner of his mouth quirked at her quick answer. "Is that decision inspired by cowardice or hunger?"

It was a little of both, but she said, "I'm just starving."

Josh smiled. "C'mon. You can help me grab a few things in the kitchen." He strode to the refrigerator, peered inside and asked, "What do you want to drink? Wine, cola, milk, juice...?"

"A cola would be great."

Still bent into the refrigerator, he glanced at her and said, "I suppose you want it in a glass over ice?"

"Well...yes."

He grinned and straightened, pulling out a couple of cans. "Plates are in that cabinet if you want to grab a couple. Tableware is in the drawer below it."

Josh snagged two glasses and held them under the refrigerator's icemaker. Over the sound of clinking ice cubes he asked, "So what do you do, Amanda? Besides chase firefighters around and organize this charity-type stuff, I mean."

Amanda had to go on tiptoe to reach the shelf of plates. In her home, she stored only the most seldom used items so high, but she supposed for a man of Josh's height, it wasn't an issue.

She began saying, "I'm a buyer for one of the mall's clothing stores—" when the telephone rang. She and

Josh both looked toward the wall unit. Neither of them moved. "Aren't you going to answer it?"

He shook his head. "The machine will pick it up."

He no sooner said that than the answering machine beeped and a woman began to speak.

*"Josh."* A wealth of disappointment rang in that utterly feminine voice. *"I was really hoping you'd be home. I miss you, baby, and you know exactly what I mean. After last week, well, let's just say I'm anxious to try that again!"*

A giggle, ripe with suggestion, made Amanda blink.

*"I need an encore, Josh, and I'm not taking no for an answer. So whatever time you get in, I don't care how late, give me a ring. I'll be here—waiting."* The woman said goodbye with a string of kissing noises and then the phone disconnected.

Amanda, feeling almost like an eavesdropper, looked at Josh.

He said, "So you're a buyer? Does that mean you get to help pick out which fashions will be most popular?"

Astounded that he intended to ignore the call, Amanda said, "Well...um..." Her mind was still back there on that *"I need an encore."* What had he done to the woman?

"I can see you being a buyer," Josh continued. "You always look really put together, so it makes sense I guess. Let's go eat. I'm starved."

Like a zombie, Amanda walked back into the dining room. Josh took the plates from her hand, held out her seat for her, and then left the room saying, "I'll be right back."

She sat there trying to gather her wits, then shook her head to clear it. She didn't care about Josh Marshall's sexual exploits! The man was such a rogue, there was no telling what the woman referred to, but no doubt it would be shocking.

With that tantalizing thought, her heart thumped hard, making her catch her breath. What type of shocking things did he indulge in?

A few seconds later a thrumming musical beat began to filter into the room from ceiling speakers. Josh reappeared just as a male singer started crooning. "You like Tom Petty?"

Since her brain was muddled, still pondering that phone call and the intimated sexuality, and she almost never listened to music anyway, Amanda merely nodded.

"Great."

Josh sauntered back to the table and began loading both plates with corn on the cob, stiff mashed potatoes and biscuits. When he reached for the chicken, Amanda said, "A breast please."

Josh glanced up, winked, and pulled out two crispy fried chicken breasts. "See, we're already finding things we have in common."

Amanda opened a paper napkin into her lap. "You think so?" After that phone call, she had serious doubts. While she avoided sexual conduct, Josh apparently embraced it.

"Absolutely." He saluted her with his glass of cola before taking a long drink. "Drinks, music and we both love breasts."

Amanda choked—and then amazingly enough, she laughed. Josh was so outrageous, it was impossible not to be entertained by him. He said and did things she'd never before imagined, much less experienced.

At the sound of her hilarity, Josh looked very pleased with himself. He sat down across from her, propped his head on a fist, and smiled. "I like your laugh," he said in a low, rough timbre.

Amanda struggled to collect herself. These spontaneous losses of decorum were not acceptable. She just couldn't seem to help herself with him. "Thank you."

"It's sexy."

Knowing she blushed, Amanda rolled her eyes. "It is not."

"Yeah," he said, searching her eyes and disconcerting her, "it is."

Refusing to be flattered, she scoffed, then shook her fork at him. "A woman can't believe anything from a man on the make."

Josh looked startled for only a moment, then he threw back his head and roared with laughter. Trying not to smile with him, Amanda ducked her head and primly, precisely broke her biscuit in half.

That only made him laugh more.

His lack of propriety was contagious, she decided, making *her* say outrageous things now. She shook her head but inside, she felt more lighthearted than she had in years.

She watched him continue to chuckle, pausing to wipe his eyes every so often and then bursting into new fits of mirth. And he kept looking at her, his expression tender and hot and happy.

No one had ever looked at her with quite that combination of feelings. Seven years ago, she'd been too young to inspire any real or complicated depth of emotion from males.

Since then, she hadn't been interested.

Finally, he dropped back into his seat, his laughter having subsided into occasional snickers. He rested his clasped hands on his hard abdomen and gave her a fond smile. "You're something else, lady, you know that?"

Something else, but *what?* She wasn't sure she wanted to know. Instead, she said, "We need you to pose for the shoot as soon as possible."

He nodded, but said, "Have lunch with me tomorrow."

With a forkful of potatoes halfway to her mouth, Amanda wavered. Did the man ever give the right answer, an answer she could anticipate? Likely not.

She put her fork down and leaned toward him. "But...we're eating now! Or rather, *I'm* eating. *You*," she accused, "are just sitting there watching me."

"I like looking at you," he said, as if it explained everything.

Amanda sat back, mimicking his pose. "Well *I* would like for you to give me some answers."

"Shoot."

That took her by surprise. She hadn't expected his ready agreement, which was probably why he gave it. "Okay." She bent a wary look on him, but his smiling expression didn't change. "When are you free to meet with the photographer?"

"My schedule rotates. I'm off tomorrow, then not again until Saturday. I regularly work ten hour days, and this week it's eight to six, so I'm really not up to photographers on a work day."

Tomorrow would be a Tuesday, less busy than a Saturday, but... "I'm not sure the photographer can do it tomorrow."

"No problem. I want to see the poses first anyway, to see what I'm getting into. I warn you, I'm not going to do anything dumb."

Amanda rushed to reassure him. "We want the men to look appealing and sexy, not dumb. You don't have to worry about that."

He looked far from reassured. "I want to see the poses."

"I don't...how?"

"Meet me tomorrow for lunch," he repeated, "and we can look over the photos you've already taken. It'll give me an idea what type of pose I want."

"The pose isn't up to you."

"Yeah," he said, "it is." He stared at her, implacable.

Amanda wanted to throw a chicken bone at him. "You're just doing this to force me to have lunch."

He neither denied nor confirmed that. "We can meet at Marcos. Are you familiar with it?"

"Yes." It was a nice family-type restaurant in the center of town, accessible from just about anywhere.

"How about noon. Does that work for you?"

"No, it does not. My lunch break is at eleven."

"Eleven's fine. I'll be there. Or would you rather I pick you up from work?"

Throwing a bone became a real possibility. "No," she groused between her teeth, "I'll meet you."

"Great. Don't be late, okay?" After all that, Josh sat forward and dug into his food.

He knew how to eat, she'd give him that. In the time it took her to eat a biscuit and about a third of her piece of chicken, he'd downed no less than two legs, a breast and a thigh, along with the remaining biscuits and potatoes and two ears of corn.

Amanda shook her head in wonder. "Do you always eat so much?"

"Lusting after you has given me an appetite."

Her mouth opened, though she wasn't sure what she'd say, and the phone rang again.

Dropping back in her seat, Amanda waited with a "here we go again" feeling of dread.

*"Josh? Are you there, sweetie? No? Well damn. I've been thinking about you, about last week and how fantastic*

*you were, and now I've gotten myself all worked up. I miss
you, Josh. Let's get together okay?"*

And then, just in case Josh hadn't understood that
blatant insinuation, she added, *"I need you. And I
promise you won't be disappointed. Bye-bye."*

Amanda rubbed her forehead.

Josh said, "You want me to see if I've got anything
for dessert? There's probably some ice cream in the
freezer, or maybe a couple of cookies."

Cookies? He hungered for snacks while women everywhere hungered for him. Without looking up she
said, "No. Thank you."

"Coffee then?"

Her throat felt tight, her stomach was in knots. Josh
was a rogue—carefree and fun loving—everything
she knew she'd never be, everything she'd learned
early on *not* to be.

Did he have women begging for his favors all the
time? Apparently, or he wouldn't be able to so easily
ignore them. She sighed. "I think I need to be heading
home, Josh."

He managed a credible look of hurt. "You mean after I bought and served dinner, you're not going to
help clean up the mess?"

Even mired in melancholy, she smiled. "Yes, all
right." Josh sat there and watched while she made
quick work of sticking the two plates, two glasses and
silverware into the dishwasher. Everything else went
into the trash can in his garage. It took her all of two
minutes, tops. "There. All done."

"I was really wanting some coffee."

His expression was that of a hopeful child, and she almost ruffled his fair hair. The man was too appealing for his own good, and he knew it.

She lifted her coat to slip it on. "We'll probably pass a place on the way back to my car that'll sell you a cup."

He stood, his movements so deliberate and precise she found herself automatically stepping back. She caught herself and stopped, bracing for his approach.

"Josh," she warned, watching him edge around the table and come closer and closer.

"Amanda." He stopped directly in front of her, making her tip her head back to see him. His stance was loose, relaxed, but his green eyes seemed warmed from within, giving away the intensity of his thoughts. A shadowing of beard stubble on his face lent the illusion of danger.

Ha! He *was* dangerous, with or without beard shadow, and Amanda knew it. So did her heart and her head—and her body.

Catching the lapels of her coat, he asked in a rough whisper, "If I kiss you, just a teeny tiny kiss, would you faint on me?"

He was so close she could smell his cologne again, mixing with the sexier earthy smell of man. Her stomach flip-flopped. "Uh..." She nodded dumbly. "It's probable."

He bent closer. "Let's see."

At the last second, Amanda remembered that this

was a game to him. He'd set out to get her in his bed as retaliation for the way she'd pestered him about the calendar. Kissing her now would only be the first step in his campaign to have sex with her.

It would be pleasurable, she had no doubts on that, but still meaningless. Never could she let that happen.

She ducked away.

Josh caught her arm and pulled her back. "Okay, I won't kiss you. But don't run from me, all right?"

She looked pointedly at his hand on her upper arm. "I can hardly run with you restraining me." She raised an eyebrow, waiting.

He had the grace to look sheepish. His hand opened wide and he held his arms out to his sides. "Sorry."

Amanda stepped aside to pull on her gloves. Her heart still raced from his nearness, from the close call. *What if she had let him kiss her?* No!

"We're not ending the night like this."

That sounded so ominous, his tone disgruntled, that she whirled around to see him, half expecting him to pounce.

Josh cursed. "Damn it, I didn't mean... Don't look at me like that. I much prefer your laughter." He ran a hand through his hair, putting it on end. "I just don't want you going home upset. I want you to understand."

"Understand what? That you intend to...to...have

your way with me, no matter what it takes and no matter what I think of it?''

His eyes glittered, one side of his mouth curled. A second later he chuckled. "Have my way with you?" He laughed again and when she scowled, he said, "Okay, okay, don't get all riled. Truth is, I want you to have your way with me. I promise not to resist too much."

"You're impossible."

"Not so." His smile epitomized masculine charm. "Hell, most women think I'm easy."

"And do they call here around the clock?" Amanda snapped her mouth shut. She wanted to choke herself, to bite off her unruly tongue, to somehow call the words back. She'd sounded petulant. She'd almost sounded...jealous. Damn.

Hoping to retreat, she held up her hands. "Never mind. I don't want to know."

"Oh, but I want to tell you." He wore a taunting smile, which perfectly matched his mussed hair and the sinful twinkle in his beautiful green eyes.

"Take me home, Josh."

"Spoilsport." His sigh was exaggerated and profound. "All right." He pulled on his leather jacket, but she saw his satisfaction. The jerk.

Once they were on the road, Josh reached for her hand. She didn't have time to evade him. He squeezed her gloved fingers and said, "Tell me you at least enjoyed part of the evening."

She shouldn't. If she gave anything away, anything at all, he'd use it against her.

"Come on, Amanda. Stop being a coward. Admit it."

"If I'm a coward then you're a bully."

"Just meet me halfway. A little admission, that's all I want. For now."

"All right, yes." She made a feeble attempt to retrieve her hand, but he didn't let go and she wasn't about to make an issue of it. "I enjoyed myself. It was a novelty."

"A novelty? You calling me odd?" He didn't sound particularly insulted.

"No, I meant going out with a man at all, eating fast food, listening to music and…laughing."

"It's been a long time since you dated?"

Thinking the truth would make him understand her resolve, she said, "Seven years."

He almost ran the car off the road. "Seven years!"

"By choice, Josh."

He fell silent for a long time. "You'd have liked the kiss, too," he eventually predicted, "if you hadn't run scared."

She believed him. There were times when she craved everything he now offered. But she'd learned the hard way that sexual frivolity could mean disaster. And she already had one disaster to make up for.

"It wasn't fear, Lieutenant. It was self-preservation. I have no intention of becoming another conquest for you."

"Those women who called?" He waited, but she refused to reply. She could hear the smile in his tone when he said, "I don't consider them conquests. That's dumb. They're just women looking for a little fun, and I'm glad to oblige them. It's a good arrangement."

"A good arrangement?" she repeated.

He shrugged. "Yeah. Casual dates, Amanda, nothing more."

She looked at him in amazement. "Casual dates do not do unspeakable things!"

His face twisted as he tried hard not to laugh, but he lost the battle. *"Unspeakable things?"* he guffawed. "Is that what you thought? Were you imagining some type of perversions in that active little mind of yours? What? Tell me Amanda. Did you think I dragged out the fire hose?" He kept laughing—at her expense.

"Shut up, Josh."

He couldn't. But he did lift her hand to his mouth to treat her knuckles to a tickling, chuckling kiss. "You are so funny. Unspeakable things." He shook his head. When they pulled up to a red light, Josh shifted toward her. "I can promise you this, Amanda honey, when I get you into my bed, you'll not consider anything we do perverted or unspeakable." His tone dropped. "You'll just enjoy yourself."

"And then I'll start calling your house begging for your favors? Don't hold your breath." She should have stopped there, but she heard herself ask, "How many women do you see anyway? A baker's dozen?"

"As of right now, only one."

Her heart plummeted. "Someone special?" Not that it should matter to her. It didn't matter to her. Her association with Josh Marshall was based strictly on the calendar. Once the photo shoot was finished she wouldn't see him again.

He pulled up next to her Beetle, put the car in park, then tugged her just a little bit closer. Looking at her mouth, he said, "Yeah, she's special." He touched her cheek, drifting his fingers down to her chin, to the sensitive skin of her throat. "And very soon, she's going to tell me all her secrets."

# 3

IT HAD BEEN the slowest morning of his life. The minutes had ticked by, and after a night fraught with erotic dreams of Ms. Amanda Barker, Josh's temperament was on the surly side.

What was she hiding?

In between those smoldering dreams of naked bodies and wet mouths and soft moans, Josh had worried. He didn't like to worry, and generally didn't waste his time with it. But that was before he'd gotten involved with Amanda.

He'd already considered every unspeakable thing that could happen to a woman and every one of them made him madder than hell. Somehow she'd been hurt, and he hoped whoever had been to blame was still around so Josh could get a piece of him.

That is, if she ever fessed up.

Just the fact that he wanted to avenge her, that he wanted to protect her, was strange for him. As strange as the damn worrying.

Whenever he'd slept, she'd occupied his thoughts. When he woke, he could think of nothing but her fear, her reservation. *Seven long years.* Incredible.

In the darkest part of the morning, when the chill

air had kept him beneath the blankets staring at the ceiling, Josh had contemplated what he'd do if Amanda never softened toward him. What if she continued to refuse him, if she wouldn't let him help, if she went on in her isolated, cold lifestyle?

What if he never even got to kiss her?

No, he wouldn't think that way. She had softened already, and he'd build on that. Last night she'd even been enjoying herself, until...

He made a sound of disgust. It had been unfortunate, those two calls coming in when they did. Amanda had relaxed enough to chat with him, to even tease him some. Then the women had called.

He was cursed with bad timing.

The restaurant was mostly empty when Josh arrived ten minutes early. He peeked in, but since he didn't see Amanda yet, he decided to wait for her by the door. The day was cool, but not overly so and the sun shone brightly. It was a day full of promise—and he intended to take advantage of it.

He was deep in sensual thoughts when a soft female hand tickled the back of his neck. Josh whirled—and came face-to-face with Vicki, one of the women who'd called the night before. He started to scowl, but then she laughed and threw herself against him.

"Josh! I fell asleep waiting for you to call me back last night! What did you do, stay out all night?"

Josh said, "No, I—"

She kissed him, her soft mouth opening on his with

determination. Josh held her back. "Vicki," he chided, "slow down." Her full-steam-ahead enthusiasm, which had first attracted him to her, now seemed a problem.

She leaned into him, pushing her full breasts into his chest, looking at him through her lashes. With one finger stroking his chin, she whispered huskily, "Come over tonight."

"I can't."

"I'll make it worth your while." Her smile made a number of promises, all of them heated.

Josh grinned. He truly loved women and the way they flirted and teased. "Sorry, babe, no can do."

Now she pouted. And Vicki's pouts were enough to bring a man to his knees. Luckily, Josh had become recently immune, thanks to Amanda.

"But why not?"

"Because as of yesterday—" he started to explain, and was interrupted from behind with a strident, "Excuse me."

Wiping the cringe off his face at that recognizable voice, Josh looked over his shoulder and sure enough, Amanda stood directly behind him, primly dressed in a soft gray business suit and matching cape, her arms stiff at her sides, her mouth set.

Despite Vicki's still tenacious hold on him, Josh smiled in pleasure at seeing her. "Amanda."

Her big brown eyes snapped with fury.

He tried to tactfully ease Vicki aside, but she held

on like a limpet. "Well," Vicki said with a predatory smile, "this is awkward."

Amanda's gaze shifted to the other woman and she said, "Not at all. You're welcome to him."

To Josh's surprise, she didn't turn on her heel and leave. No, she shoved her way around him and went into the restaurant.

It took him a few seconds and then he started chuckling. She was jealous! And not just a little jealous, but outright furious with it.

It was more than he'd dared hope for. The night before, he'd suspected, but her performance today left no doubts. He looked at Vicki and gave her a quick hard smooch on the lips.

"She's jealous," he said, still grinning like the village idiot.

Vicki peered at him askance. "I was...um, under the impression you didn't like jealous women."

"Amanda is special," he told her by way of an explanation.

"She is?"

"Yes." And then gently, "That's what I was just about to tell you. I'm officially out of commission. No more dating."

Her jaw loosened. "You're kidding."

"Sorry, no." It was all Josh could do to keep from laughing. Oh, some men might run from the sudden idea of getting pulled from the dating scene, but not him. Hell, he'd spent all his life playing around. He'd enjoyed himself and he was pretty sure the women he'd been with would say the same. He had no regrets. But now...Amanda affected him differently. She was different.

He thought of Mick and Zack, how they'd gotten involved recently. Mick had already married Delilah, and Zack and Wynonna had set a date. But before that, both men had fought the inevitable tooth and nail, to the point they'd almost messed things up.

Josh considered himself smarter than that. He'd been with enough women to know what he felt around Amanda was different and unique. As he'd told Vicki, special.

He wouldn't blow it. No way.

Vicki frowned at him, looking like someone had just goosed her. He gave her an apologetic shrug. "I'm sure you understand why you shouldn't call anymore, and why we can't be standing here in the walkway like this."

"No, actually I don't understand." She searched his face, then put the back of her hand to his forehead. "You're not acting like yourself, Josh. Are you okay?"

Josh set her aside. He almost rubbed his hands together, thinking of his plans. More to himself than Vicki, he said, "There's a good chance this might work out with Amanda. I don't want to blow it by fooling around. As you just witnessed, she doesn't like the idea of me with other women."

"And that matters to you? Her likes and dislikes?"

"Of course it does."

Josh decided he'd make a few calls that night, let

the women he still saw know that he wasn't available anymore. He'd give Amanda all his considerable concentration. It'd have to be enough.

Having made up his mind, he nodded to Vicki. "I need to get inside. The longer she sits there, the more she'll stew and the longer she'll want to make me suffer."

Still wary of his sudden turnaround, Vicki said, "Well, okay. But if you change your mind..."

"I won't."

She shook her head. "Good luck then." She gave him another brief hug and left.

Good luck indeed, Josh thought, peeking into Marcos and seeing Amanda staring stonily toward him. Had she watched the whole exchange in the doorway, and seen that last farewell hug? Probably. She sat at a round table in the corner, and she didn't look happy.

Josh shoved his hands into his pockets and sauntered in. He almost whistled, but he thought that might be overdoing it. When he reached the table, Amanda snapped open her menu, using it to hide behind.

Josh dropped into his seat. She was so adorable. And so damn vulnerable. And *so* incredibly hot. "I hope you're hungry, because I'm ravenous."

She harrumphed.

"Yeah," he said, trying to gauge her mood. "about that woman I was with outside..."

"Not my business."

Her words were brisk and cold and, damn it, he couldn't help himself. He liked it that she was piqued. He sat back in his seat, crossed his arms over his chest, and said, "I told her I was unavailable now."

Amanda slapped the menu down. "You did *what?*"

"I told her I was—"

"I heard that," she snapped impatiently. "Why would you tell her such an idiotic thing?"

Josh slid his foot over next to hers. The long table-cloths on the round tables hid their legs, and gave him the opportunity to play footsies. He rubbed his ankle against hers. Amanda's eyes rounded and she jumped, making him smile.

He was willing to bet Amanda had never played footsies under the table.

He was willing to bet there was a lot she hadn't done, *and thinking that would definitely give him a boner*, so he brought his mind back to more important issues. "I told you I was only seeing one woman right now."

She denied that with a hard shake of her head. "Not me."

"Yeah, you."

"Josh, no." The pulse in her throat fluttered and her hands flattened on the tabletop. "Once the calendar is complete, there'll be no reason for me to see you again."

He didn't like the sound of that at all. "Unacceptable."

She drew back like a verbal prizefighter, ready to go for the knockout—and luckily the waiter stepped forward. "What can I get you folks to drink?"

Amanda sputtered. Josh slid in smoothly with, "Coffee for me. Amanda?"

Her teeth clinked together. She glared at the hapless waiter, then muttered, "Ice water."

"*Only* ice water?" Josh questioned.

Without looking at him, she said again to the hovering waiter, enunciating sharply, "*Ice—water.*"

"Yes ma'am. I'll get your drinks right away."

Josh chuckled. "You terrorized that poor boy."

"I did not."

"Look at him."

She glanced toward the kitchen area where the waiter whispered to another while gesturing with his hands. Both young men glanced at her, then quickly dashed away, trying to look busy, when they saw they had her attention.

Amanda moaned. She propped her head up with her hands and said, "You're such a bad influence."

"Blaming me for your nasty temper?" He pretended a grave affront. "*Tsk tsk.* Not fair, sweetheart. In case you haven't noticed, I'm in a cheerful mood."

Rather than comment on his mood, and why he was cheerful, she said, "I am *not* your sweetheart."

"Not yet anyway. But I'm working on it." It was a good thing they were in a public place, Josh thought.

He had no doubt she'd just mentally bashed him real good.

"I never had a nasty temper before meeting up with you."

"I noticed." He said it kindly, with a measure of sympathy. "You kinda worked in one gear, didn't you? Bland."

"Controlled," she grumbled through her teeth. "Polite. Mannerly, considerate, respectful..."

Josh laughed. Riling her was so easy, he could hardly credit that he'd ever believed her prudish or bland. "Okay! I get the picture. So I bring out the beast in you, huh?"

"Unfortunately, yes." Her fingernails, today painted a rosy almost-red, tapped on the tabletop. "Actually, I thought about that last night."

"About me?" Now they were getting somewhere.

"This is not a reason to be hopeful, Josh. I thought about how horribly I'd behaved, how I'm going to have to work doubly hard to maintain an even keel around you."

The bottom dropped out of his stomach. She sounded so serious, so self-castigating. "I wish you wouldn't." And before she could go into another cold explanation, he added, "I thought about you a lot last night, too. About how nice it was to hear you laugh and see you being just a little bit devilish. Much nicer than when you're working so hard to be refined and unemotional."

"I have my reasons."

"I wish you'd share them with me."

"I doubt they'd make any difference to a man like you."

Now that was an insult he couldn't ignore. "A man like me, huh? Why don't you explain that."

A stony expression had entered her eyes. "I care about the calendar, about those less fortunate who'll benefit by the proceeds. I would think with you being a firefighter, you'd be especially empathetic also."

His face muscles felt too tight to allow him to speak, but he managed. "What makes you think I'm not? What gives you the right to judge me?"

A moment of uncertainly flashed over her features. "You wanted nothing to do with the calendar."

"I see. And your project is the only way to help? Money and time can't be donated directly? There aren't other projects going on?"

Just like that, she paled. Guilt, heavy and ugly, visibly weighed her down. "You do all those things?"

He'd said too much. God knew, he hadn't wanted to upset her, to bring on such a pained expression. He flattened his mouth in self-disgust, and reached for her hand.

In turn, she reached for a leather case by her seat and he was left grasping air. Josh retreated as she extracted a folder. In a small, apologetic voice, she said, "I brought the photos you requested."

"Amanda."

"You can look them over and see which ones you like."

He ignored the glossy eight-by-ten photographs. "You're right that my job makes me more sensitive to some issues, especially concerning burn victims."

Face averted, she rushed to say, "We don't need to talk about this."

"I've seen the reality of what a burn victim suffers, how his life is affected."

"Josh please." She looked around the restaurant as if seeking help.

Josh frowned, and pressed her despite her upset. *He had to know.* "Why are you so concerned, baby? Explain it to me."

She exploded. Hands flat on the table, voice elevated enough to draw attention, she all but shouted, "I am *not* your baby! I will never be your damned baby!"

So much bottled emotion, so much she kept repressed. Josh tickled his fingertips up her wrist to her elbow. "I figure your jealousy is a good sign. At the very least I know you're not being honest when you say you're uninterested."

Her face frozen, she fanned out the pictures, slapping them into place one by one, and growled, "As you can see, the photos are done in bright, eye-catching colors with natural backdrops—"

"The way I see it, once you tell me what your hangups are, we can work on getting past them." *God, let him be able to get her past them.* He now had a few suspicions and consequently his stomach was in knots and it felt like his heart had cramped.

Gently, with loads of reassurance, he added, "I'm willing to be patient, by the way, if you need some time for that. It'll make me nuts, because I want you really bad, but I figure you're worth the wait."

One of the pictures tore in her hands. She stared at it, appalled. "Look what you made me do."

"You have other copies?"

She nodded. "Yes. And it's already been sent to the printer anyway. But..."

The waiter cautiously approached. "Um...I have your drinks and if you're ready to order..."

Josh scooped up the photos. Amanda looked a little numb and he soothed her by rubbing his thumb on the inside of her delicate wrist.

She jerked back. "I'll have the soup and a salad with lo-cal Italian dressing."

"Yes, ma'am." The waiter hastily scribbled down her order, anxious, no doubt, to escape once again. The tension at the table was thick enough to choke on.

He looked at Josh.

"A burger, loaded, double order of fries, and a chocolate malt." He eyed Amanda. "You sure you don't want something more than soup?"

She appeared too dazed to answer, so Josh closed the menus and said quietly to the waiter, "That'll be it."

The waiter escaped with alacrity.

Josh sought her small feet out again and enclosed them in both of his, making sure she couldn't escape. Amanda looked up at him.

"It's okay you know."

"No." She shook her head and her eyes looked shiny with dazed confusion. "It's not okay."

"Why?" He reached for her hand and amazingly enough, she let him enfold her fingers in his own. She even gripped him tightly.

"You're making me muddled, Josh. I don't want to be muddled."

"Muddled is good. It means you're maybe just a little bit as affected by all this as me."

"All this?"

She looked skeptical again. "Sexual chemistry, instant attraction, whatever you want to call it."

Regaining some of her old self, she scoffed. "Do I really look that naïve, Josh, that stupid? Or have you forgotten you already told me what you want and why? A little retaliation, a little payback because I was too persistent in getting you involved with the calendar."

"That is what I wanted—at first."

"Oh, and now you've suddenly got more altruistic motives?"

"No, now I know you a little better and I've smelled you and laughed with you, and I want you. Just because you're sexy as hell and you turn me on and because in some strange skewed way, your laugh is almost more exciting than sex with other women."

Her face flamed. She almost choked, swallowed a large drink of her water, then said, "You *smelled* me?"

Covering his grin, Josh pressed his thumb to the

racing pulse in her wrist and said, "The smell of your skin makes me hard. I want to get you naked and smell you all over, everywhere. I want to rub myself against you until our two scents mix."

She went mute.

Josh leaned across the table and lowered his voice to a barely-there whisper. "Do you know what you smell like, Amanda?"

She shook her head and stared at his mouth.

Damn, he thought, seeing her skin rosy with warmth, her eyes darkened. He wanted to kiss her, right here, right now.

He had a feeling she'd let him.

So what did he care if they were in a public place, if other patrons saw them? *He didn't.* They'd already seen them arguing, so now they'd just think they'd made up.

Besides, he ate at Marcos regularly with Mick and Zack. Most everyone there already knew him, so they'd understand.

Josh slowly moved closer to her, watching her lips part, seeing her tongue move behind her teeth, and...

"Hey Josh." A hard thwack on his shoulder almost took him out of his chair.

Josh straightened with a wince. Mick and Zack stood there, smiling down at him.

"Go away."

Amanda gasped.

Josh shook his head at her. "Don't worry, they won't think I'm rude."

"Of course we will," Zack disagreed, and pulled a chair from another table to join them. "Hey, Ms. Barker. How are you doing?"

"Fine." Her voice squeaked and she cleared her throat. "How are you, Mr. Grange?"

Josh stared at one of his best friends. "You know Amanda?"

"Sure I do. We've spoken several times."

Amanda looked flushed. "I wanted Mr. Grange to pose for the calendar, too. I know he's a paramedic, but he does work for the fire department. With his excellent physique and good looks, he'd have been perfect."

Zack chuckled. "Don't you just love how she states all that without leering? Too bad it never worked out." He said that tongue in cheek, because Josh knew exactly how Zack would feel about posing in a beefcake photo. "I had all that overtime, remember?"

Josh remembered that he'd volunteered for a load of overtime just recently.

Mick, too, pulled up a chair, turning it around and sitting with his arms braced on the chair back. "Hi. I'm Mick Dawson, a friend of theirs, too."

She nodded. "Hello." She looked Mick over with professional interest. "Hmmm. I never saw you at the fire station. Are you a firefighter, a paramedic? Either way, we could have really used you on the calendar, too."

Josh rolled his eyes. "Amanda, please stop telling

all my friends how sexy and gorgeous you think they are. It's embarrassing."

Zack snickered. "For you maybe."

Amanda, red-faced with embarrassment, threw her spoon at him. It bounced off his chest. Josh caught it, grinned and handed it back to her.

"I'm with the police," Mick interjected, regaining Amanda's notice before a war broke out. "Undercover."

Amanda looked awed at that information. "Undercover!"

Josh spread his arms wide. "Gee, why don't you guys join us?"

His sarcasm was completely ignored. "Thanks," Zack said, then asked, "What's with the pics?"

Amanda cleared her throat yet again, though she kept sneaking peeks at Mick. Josh was used to that. Mick was so dark, an air of mystery just clung to him, attracting women for miles. Amazingly, Mick had been mostly oblivious to them all—until Delilah invaded his life. Then he'd fallen hard.

While peering at Mick, Amanda's blush intensified, but now her expression was clear of any sexual interest. If anything, she looked more remote than ever. "The lieutenant has finally agreed to pose for the calendar," she explained to Zack, "but he wanted to see some of the various shots first."

Mick snatched them out of Josh's hand and flipped through them. After he looked at each picture, he handed it across the table to Zack. Together they "hmmed" and "hummed" to the point of real irritation.

"They're all ridiculous," Josh grumbled, feeling a little ill at ease. "Firemen do not work without shirts or helmets. That's just plain stupid. Why aren't any of them in real uniform? Where's the turn-out gear? The steel-toed boots?"

Amanda made an impatient sound. "We wanted them to look sexy."

"Yeah, well no one cares how sexy they look when they're putting out a damn fire. There's no helmets, no Nomex hoods, and not a single S.C.B.A."

Zack shrugged. "The calendar isn't meant as a career description. It's just for fun."

"Fun? Did you see this one? The guy has his bunker coat on, but it's hanging open to show off his *shaved* chest." Josh grunted in disgust. "Wouldn't do him a damn lot of good that way would it?"

Zack turned to Amanda and excused Josh's surly mood by saying, "Being the lieutenant and all, he has to take his responsibility to the crew pretty serious."

"You know," Mick interjected, putting the remaining photos aside, "I've seen Josh at a fire when he's pulled on his bunker gear right over his underwear." In a lower, confiding voice, he added, "You know— *no* uniform."

"Yeah," Zack said, nodding. "He does do that a lot. And after he finishes with the call, he has a habit of jerking off his jacket and strutting around all dirty and bare-chested with his suspenders loose enough

that you think his pants are going to fall right off."
Zack leaned toward Amanda, who leaned away.
"Josh has a hairy chest, not like the Romeo in the
photo. I think he likes showing it off."

"I do not strut," Josh said. Since Amanda had already seen him in the locker room wearing nothing
more than a towel, she was intimately aware of his
hairy chest so he didn't comment on that. "And I take
off my jacket when the job is done because it's usually
hotter than Hades and we're roasting in our own
sweat."

"The civilian females are always whispering about
him. They—*ouch!*" Mick reached beneath the table to
rub his ankle. "Damn it, that hurt."

Josh thought about kicking him again. "Shut the
hell up, will you?"

"Why?" Zack asked. "She already knows your reputation. Any woman who's been around you ten
minutes sees how it is, and she's been around you
longer than that."

Almost on cue, three women at another table
laughed conspicuously and when Josh looked up, he
saw they were staring at him. One even gave a flirtatious, three-finger wave.

Amanda shoved back her chair and threw her napkin on the table. "I think I need to visit the ladies'
room."

Josh, Mick and Zack all lurched to their feet with
gentlemanly haste.

"You *think?*" Josh asked, seeing that she once again

looked jealous. It gave him hope, that very human emotion meant she cared. "You don't know for sure?"

"Oh...be quiet." Spine military straight, she marched away, and the men reseated themselves.

Mick and Zack peered questioningly at Josh, who just grinned. "She'll be back," he said, "after she composes herself."

Mick whistled low. "Wow. She looked ready to bite your face off."

Zack said, "I've never seen her in a temper. Whenever she's been around the station, she's always been so..." He searched for a word and finally settled on, "Cool."

Josh shook his head. "That's just a front."

"It is?"

"Yeah. She's actually a very warm woman. And she doesn't like other women flirting with me."

"Is that what set her off?" Zack lifted a mocking brow. "Because I thought maybe it was the way you harangued her about the calendar. After all, it's her pet project, and you, my friend, just ran it into the ground."

Josh froze. His stomach cramped, even his brain cramped. For a man who professed to know women, he'd blown that one. He wanted to kick himself in the backside. "*Shit.*"

Mick snickered.

As soon as Amanda presented herself again, he'd make it up to her. He'd explain why he was sensitive on the subject, and maybe, just maybe, she'd confide a little about her own sensitivities.

He saw Zack nudge Mick in shared amusement, and he asked, "What are you two doing here anyway?"

Zack held out his hands in a placating gesture. "We came for lunch. We haven't gotten together in a month."

Mick shook his head. "Hard to believe we used to manage a regular get-together, what? At least once a week, right?"

"We were pathetic," Zack agreed.

Because Zack and Mick had seldom dated, they'd had plenty of time to meet at Marcos. Mick was a natural loner who trusted very few people, and Zack had a four-year-old daughter who normally took up all his time. Until they'd met the right women, they'd made meeting at Marcos for lunch a highlight of the week.

Josh, as a once confirmed free-wheeling lady's man, hadn't been bothered with any commitments other than ones he arranged himself, so he'd been able to adjust his schedule around theirs. Being with his buddies had been important to him—then.

Now he wished they'd disappear.

"What's Delilah doing?"

Mick rolled his eyes. "She's interviewing a bunch of prostitutes down on State Street."

"*What?*" As a writer, Delilah Piper-Dawson engaged in a lot of strange research, but usually Mick was at her side, protecting her whether she needed protection or not. At one point in time, Josh had entertained a secret infatuation for her. She was the type of woman who told it straight and charmed a man in the process. But then Mick had fallen in love with her, and she adored Mick from first sight, so Josh had forced himself to think of her only in platonic terms.

"It's all right," Zack assured him. "Wynn went with her and besides, the women are reformed prostitutes Mick busted months ago. They're nice ladies—with a wealth of information to share."

At nearly six feet tall with strength far surpassing that of most females, Wynn Lane could serve as protection, Josh supposed. But she was still a woman, still very female in the most important ways—ways he sure as hell couldn't help but notice.

He thought his two friends about as lucky as men could get. "One of you asses should have gone along."

"They wouldn't let us," Zack replied.

Mick nodded in agreement. "They said the women wouldn't be as open with us around."

Josh shook his head in pity. "You're both whipped."

Zack slapped a hand to his heart and sighed. "Happily so, yeah."

Envy gripped him. Josh wanted to be that happy, damn it, and he wanted Amanda. After meeting Delilah and Wynn, he'd thought he wanted a woman like them—tall with mile-long legs, outgoing, ballsy and honest to a fault.

Instead, he'd gotten thrown for a loop by a tiny, prissed-up woman with well-hidden secrets and a definite lack of attraction for sex.

What the hell was taking her so long?

Here he was, worrying again, and that was enough to make any man crazed. He heard himself mutter, "She doesn't want anything to do with me."

Mick and Zack shared a look. "Who?"

"Of all the stupid questions! *Amanda.*" They looked as incredulous as he often felt, so Josh nodded. "It's true. I've had to coerce every single second out of her. If it wasn't for her damned project, she wouldn't be here with me now."

"She's not attracted to you?" Zack asked, forcing Josh to admit the awful truth again.

"No. And I don't like it."

"No man would."

At that moment, Amanda came rushing back to the table. Her animosity had been replaced with excitement. "I just got a call!" She waved her cell phone at Josh. "The photographer had a cancellation. We can do the shoot today."

Josh was so stunned he forgot to stand. "Today?"

Mick held her chair out for her, and Zack took her arm as he seated her.

Josh thought about clouting them both.

"Yes. At six." She dropped back in her seat, all smiles again. "That'll give me enough time to finish up at work, and you'll be able to go to the station to pick up your gear."

Still feeling slow, Josh asked, "My gear?"

"Of course. For ambiance. You and I can meet at the park at five-thirty, by the nature trails. That way we can get set up before the photographer arrives."

She seemed to have everything all figured out and simply assumed he'd go along with her. As if he didn't have a life, as if he were at her beck and call.

Which, at the moment, he was.

Disturbed by that reality, Josh almost lied and said he had other plans. But one look at the excitement on her face, and he knew he couldn't disappoint her.

"I have the perfect image in mind," she told him.

Josh looked at Mick and then at Zack. They both shrugged, unable to offer any help.

"The perfect image?" he asked.

She nodded. "I know exactly what I want."

Josh closed his eyes. He knew what she wanted, too, and it wasn't him, damn it. But he liked seeing her smile too much to *not* do it. And this way he'd get to spend more of the day with her.

He opened his eyes, accepting his fate and not all that displeased with it. He grinned. "All right. I'll do it."

"Thank you."

"There's a small catch."

# 4

AMANDA CROSSED her arms and stared stonily out the windshield. What kind of stupid "catch" was this? "I don't know why we couldn't bring both cars."

"Because if I'm going to do this," he explained, not the least bothered by her mood, "I at least want to get to spend time with you."

She wouldn't explain to him again. Sooner or later he'd give up. Intimacy was not in her future, whether she wished it or not. That part of her had been permanently frozen seven years ago, thanks to stupid mistakes and irresponsibility.

She said, "I like your friends."

"Mick and Zack?"

"Yes." She twisted toward him. "Tell me about their wives."

"Mick is the only one married so far. Zack has to work around his daughter and Wynn's nutty family." He glanced at her and smiled. "No easy feat that. If you ever met her family, you'd understand."

"He doesn't get along with them?"

"Sure he does. Everyone likes Zack. He's so easy-going and all. Well, he wasn't always easygoing around Wynn. In fact, she kicked his ass a few times."

Amanda said, "Right."

"No, she did. Wynn is a lot of woman." He wore a
secret little sexy smile as he said that. "Almost six feet
tall—with the longest most incredible legs you'll ever
see. She's strong, and outgoing and athletic."

Admiration dripped from his tone, making
Amanda want to grind her teeth.

"Zack got thrown to his back more than once.
Course, letting a woman get you on your back isn't always a bad thing." He bobbed his eyebrows suggestively. "I personally think Zack knew exactly what he
was doing all along."

Amanda couldn't conceive of a woman wrestling
with a man. It seemed much too farfetched, like
something out of a sideshow. "You sound very taken
with her."

"Wynn? Yeah, sure. She's great. I suppose if Zack
hadn't involved himself, I might have asked her out."

Amanda stiffened; he hadn't even bothered to
deny it! "Does Zack know how you feel?"

"How I *felt*, and sure he did. I rubbed it in every
chance I could, just to keep him on his toes." He
smiled at her. "A little competition is good for a guy.
Besides, Wynn never gave me a second look, except
when she wanted to ask me questions about Zack."

Amanda didn't want to hear any more about the
amazing amazon who Josh respected and liked so
much. "What about Mr. Dawson? You said he's married."

"To Delilah Piper. You ever heard of her?"

She shook her head. "Should I have?"

"She's a popular mystery writer. A real sweetheart with a twisted imagination, which I guess comes in handy when she's writing those awesome stories." He shuddered. "The stuff she does in the name of research is enough to make a man crazed."

Locking her teeth, Amanda ground out, "You sound rather partial to her, too."

"Yeah." He said that so softly, she wanted to thwack him. "I fancied myself in love with her for a while. But again, she set her sights on Mick and that was all she wrote."

"Do you make a habit of trying to seduce your friends' girlfriends?"

"Nope."

He didn't elaborate. Amanda stewed for a few minutes in silence until she realized why she was stewing. God, it was ridiculous for her to even entertain such ideas of envy. She'd learned the hard way that anything beyond casual acquaintance with a man was impossible.

Josh pulled into the entrance for the park and slowed the car. As he maneuvered the winding roads toward the walking trails, he reached for Amanda's hand.

"I used to think I wanted a woman like them. Just goes to show we never really know our own minds."

Amanda felt her heart flutter and called herself a fool. "What do you mean?"

He pulled up to a gravel lot and parked the car.

Turning toward her, he said, "These days, there's only one woman plaguing my thoughts. And she's nothing like Wynn or Del."

Amanda drew her own comparisons. They sounded like wonderful women who led exciting, normal lives. They sounded like women who relished their sexuality and gave with all their hearts.

Her heart was encased in a layer of guilt, crushed under the burden of reparation.

She drew an unsteady breath. "Let's try to get set up before Jerry arrives."

"Jerry is the photographer?"

"Yes." Josh had picked her up at her home and together they'd gone to the station. One thing she'd insisted he bring along was his ax. He'd mumbled and grumbled and done as she asked.

She hadn't been quite so accommodating.

When he picked her up, he'd wanted to get out and look at her house, but she'd been waiting at the end of the long drive and hadn't invited him any farther. Because the trees on the property were thick, even when barren of leaves, and the driveway winding, he hadn't really seen anything at all. Her unusual little whimsical home was nobody's business but her own.

"Don't forget the ax," she reminded him when he left it behind on the floor of the back seat. He rasped something she couldn't hear, and she smiled. "Here, I'll take your pants. You can leave your bunker jacket and helmet behind for now." No way would she cover up his gorgeous face or magnificent body any more than absolutely necessary. "Bring your boots, though."

She walked away, not waiting to hear Josh's reaction to her directions. She peered up at the beautiful blue sky and hoped Jerry got there on time because the sun would soon be fading.

She found a spot on the ground with no grass and bent down, careful not to soil her suit. Josh reached her just as she finished rubbing the front and back and especially the knees of his once clean pants into the dirt.

He didn't ask, so she turned to look up at him and said, "They were too clean. We want you to look like you've been working."

"Firemen don't roll around in the dirt."

She hid a smile; he could be so prickly at times. "Believe me, I know exactly what it is firemen do."

Speculation darkened his green eyes. "Had first-hand experience have you?"

Rather than meet his gaze or answer his question, she stood and shook out the pants. They now looked well worn. "Here, put these on."

Allowing her the evasion, Josh looked around. There weren't many people in the park this time of year, certainly not so far back near the trails. He asked with sinful suggestiveness, "Over my jeans, or not?"

She knew he wanted her to gasp and blush, but she'd already made up her mind about the shot, so she said simply, "Not."

He cocked out his hip, bunched the heavy pants in

one fist, and glared at her. "You want me to skin out my jeans right here?"

"There's no one watching. If you're shy, then you can step behind that large tree. But hurry. I want you ready when Jerry arrives." No way did she want to try to organize another session with Josh. More than anything, she needed to get away from him. He tempted her, when she knew from experience there was no point.

He didn't go behind a tree. No, not Josh Marshall. He stared her in the eye while he kicked off his shoes and unhooked his belt.

*Now* she blushed.

"No, don't run off," he taunted. "I'll need you to hold my jeans. That is, if you can refrain from grinding them into the dirt."

Amanda assumed a casual pose. "Fine. But hurry it up." She'd already seen him, she reminded herself. The shock of that first viewing still haunted her at night—so what was a little more haunting for such a worthy cause?

He shoved his jeans down to his ankles and stepped out of them. Luckily, the shirttails of his flannel covered everything of interest.

It had been dry lately, leaving the hard ground cold but thankfully not wet. His socks would have been soaked otherwise.

A car pulled into the lot. They both turned, but to Amanda's dismay, it wasn't Jerry.

Mick and Zack stepped out, identical expressions

of hilarity on their faces when they spied Josh in his underwear. They laughed while trying to keep two women stuck in the car.

Amanda watched as one slender, almost fragile woman with incredible dark hair slipped out to stand beside Mick. She wore sloppy jeans, an unbuttoned corduroy coat over an enormous sweater, and a fat smile. She took one look at Josh and gave a loud appreciative wolf whistle—destroying the image of frail femininity.

On the driver's side of the car, Zack got shoved aside and a veritable giant of a woman emerged. She wore gray sweats, no coat and had the fuzziest hair Amanda had ever seen. Raising her long arms into the air, she applauded, then yelled, "Hey, don't let us stop you, Josh! Keep going."

Josh laughed. "This is all I'm taking off, you lecher."

Amanda felt as if she'd faded into the background. An easy camaraderie existed between the five people, a nearly palpable friendship that excluded her. She crossed her arms under her breasts and tried not to feel resentful.

These people deserved happiness. Unlike her, these people hadn't committed any terrible transgressions.

Still without pants, Josh nearly felled her when he threw his muscled arm around her shoulders and urged her forward. "Wynn, Del, I want you to meet

Amanda Barker. She's doing this crazy benefit calendar and I'm her newest victim."

The word victim echoed through Amanda's head with painful clarity. From somewhere deep inside, she dredged up a polite smile and met the two paragons who had nearly stolen Josh's heart. "Hello."

Del stepped forward and embraced her. "Hey, I'm Del, Mick's wife and a friend of Josh. Sorry if we're intruding, but Wynn and I finished our business and had the rest of the day free and Josh and Mick insisted on coming here to stick their noses in, so naturally we had to tag along, too."

She'd said all that without taking a breath and Amanda's brain whirled. "No, that is, I don't mind as long as Josh doesn't care."

Zack cuddled his big wife into his side. "Doesn't matter if he cares, we don't pay him any mind anyway."

With a beautiful smile, Wynn reached out her hand. "I'm Wynn, Zack's soon-to-be wife if we can ever get everything arranged."

"Where's Dani?" Josh asked.

Wynn said, "With my mother. They're doing some tie-dye. She'll have Dani looking like a hippie in no time."

Zack just laughed and explained, "Dani is my daughter, four years old going on forty. It took her all of about five minutes to get Wynn and her entire family wrapped around her little finger."

"And when he says little, he means little," Wynn

added. "Dani is a tiny little thing. I feel like a giant around her."

Amanda wondered that the woman ever *didn't* feel like a giant. Not that her height mattered, because she was lovely even with that awful hair that kept dancing in the wind like dandelion fluff. The loose sweats couldn't quite hide all her curves—Wynn had a body like a model.

Amanda caught herself standing there stupidly with everyone looking at her, and she said, "Oh, I was just telling Josh how we'd do the shoot." She turned and shoved the soiled pants at him. "Here, you can put these on now." The man had absolutely no shame, lounging around without pants.

Grinning, Mick said, "It is kinda cool today to be out here in your drawers."

While Josh pulled on the pants, Amanda fetched his boots. She hated awkward silences and explained, "His is the last picture we need and we'll use it for the cover and other promo, too. I want a candid shot of him without a shirt, holding his ax, maybe with a small smile."

Wynn said, "Josh does have a very nice smile."

Josh blew a kiss toward her, then grunted when Amanda shoved the boots at his midsection, making him scramble to grab them. He looked at her and laughed—the jerk.

Realizing what she'd done, Amanda peered up at the women and caught them watching her with gleeful expectation, curiosity and consideration.

Thank God, Jerry arrived.

Amanda rushed to greet him and help him with his equipment while Josh donned the steel-toed boots. Normally, she knew, the boots were already in place at the bottom of the pants. The firefighters stepped into their pants and boots at the same time, making it easier and quicker to dress.

There was nothing "normal" about this particular day. "I'm so glad you're here, Jerry. I know you're not late or anything, but I was afraid we'd lose the light. And Josh is antsy. I don't know how much longer we have before he storms away. He's not always the most agreeable man about this stuff. Not at all like the other firefighters we've been working with."

Amanda realized she was babbling and snapped her mouth shut.

Jerry gave her a long look. "No worries. I take a lot of outdoor pictures in less light than this. Like most photographers—" he bobbed his bushy brows "—I have special cameras and lenses with me. It'll be fine."

She tried to busy herself by pulling a leather bag out of Jerry's car and he said, "Hey, hey, easy with that, okay? Just let me get it."

Flustered, Amanda moved out of his way.

Jerry was a large man, thick through the middle with a drooping mustache and balding head. Though he seldom rushed, he always looked flushed with exertion. Even now, he wore only a pullover without a jacket yet he appeared overheated.

Laden with equipment, Jerry turned and surveyed the collection of people. He frowned. "So who's our model today?"

They all pointed at Josh.

Jerry huffed and lumbered across the lawn. "Off with the shirt then." He dug into a bag and pulled out a small can of something. "For the photo, Ms. Barker wants it to appear as if you've just been on the job. Very macho stuff, you know."

Josh's jaw tightened, but he did tug off his shirt and threw it toward Mick, who caught it handily. He stood there in only the pants and boots. His suspenders hung at his side, and the waistband to the bunker pants was loose, curling outward to show his navel and a downy trail of hair on his abdomen.

Amanda forced her gaze upward, to safer, but no less tempting ground.

Gooseflesh had already arisen on his arms. The air had a definite nip, but Amanda assured herself it would only take a few minutes to get the picture. Josh was a big man layered in muscle. He'd be fine.

"I've got some blackening here," Jerry announced. "We'll rub it all around on you, your chest, arms, neck, maybe even your gut, dirty you up a bit so you match those scruffy pants and then I'll spray you with baby oil to simulate sweat, and voilà, a hard workin' man."

Jerry carefully set all his equipment on a nearby

picnic table then opened the jar. He started toward Josh and Josh said, "No damn way."

Jerry wavered. He looked at Amanda, one bushy brow elevated.

Amanda looked at Josh. He stood braced as if for combat, jaw jutting slightly forward, eyes narrowed, his arms loose but fisted at his sides, his feet braced apart, his stomach tight.

She stomped forward. Her high heels sank into the ground with the ferocity of her pique. "Josh," she hissed close to him, "you agreed."

Green eyes glittering, he said, "I never once agreed to have some guy smear black stuff on me."

"Only a little," Jerry explained, oblivious to the static tension in the air. "It won't take much."

Josh shook his head. "Hell no."

"I need you to look like you've been working," Amanda insisted.

He glared at Jerry while replying to her. "I've never in my life had a guy rub me down and I'll be damned if I'm going to start now."

Mick choked and Zack guffawed. Even Wynn and Delilah began chuckling.

Amanda wanted to shout at them all; their hilarity didn't help the situation. Despite Jerry's assurances, she wanted to make use of the remaining light. She could just picture Josh with a halo of crimson sunshine behind him.

She wanted everyone else to see him as she saw him.

She was in far too deep and she knew it.

"Fine," she said, refusing to dwell on her growing admiration for Josh. "You can rub it on yourself."

He gave one hard shake of his head. "No way. I don't want my hands in that goo."

Wynn shouted, "Oh for pity's sake, *I'll* do it." She started forward, her long legs eating up the distance in record time.

Amanda whirled on her just as Zack snagged her by the seat of her pants. "*No*," Amanda said.

"*No*," Zack said.

It was a contest who frowned more, Zack or Amanda. Left with few choices, Amanda snatched the jar from Jerry's hand and stuck her fingers into the greasy goo. No way would she let one of the paragons touch Josh's naked flesh, not now, not right here in front of her. The slick inky gunk went between her fingers and beneath her manicured nails. She wrinkled her nose in distaste.

Then she looked at Josh's magnificent chest.

"Hold still," she grumbled at him, seeing that he now looked triumphant.

"I won't move a muscle," Josh promised, and then he held his arms out to the sides, his muscles going all rigid and tight as he waited for her touch.

With a fortifying deep breath that did her no good at all, Amanda smoothed in the first dark smear, right across his pectoral muscle. Despite the late October weather and the lateness of the day, he felt warm. And hard. And...sexy.

God, she hadn't learned a thing. Every moral reparation that she'd fought to gain over the past seven years had been obliterated by Josh Marshall. Now what was she supposed to do?

Josh watched Amanda, knowing he'd end up aroused but not giving a damn. She looked adorable. With fierce concentration, she watched the movements of her hand on his body as she smeared the blackening here and there. It wouldn't take much imagination on his part to visualize her making love with that same degree of intense focus.

He shivered.

Amanda glanced up and in a low, slightly raspy voice, she asked, "Are you cold?"

He answered in kind, every bit as affected as she. "You're touching me, sweetheart. I'm getting hotter by the second."

Her lips parted.

Jerry said, "Put a little on his abdomen, around all those macho muscles. Highlight 'em a bit."

Amanda looked down at Josh's stomach and hesitated.

"Go ahead," Josh encouraged her, wanting her hands on him even if they had a damned attentive audience. Mick and Zack would give him hell the rest of the month, but he could live with it.

She swallowed, and dipped her delicate hand back into the can. Her fingers and the goo felt cool against his heated skin. Hoping she wouldn't notice too much, Josh put his hands on her shoulders in the guise of steadying her. Their foreheads almost touched as they both watched the progress of her fingers caressing him.

Jerry made an impatient sound. "Hey, you two. If we're not going to take pictures after all, then at least go get a room."

Mick and Zack howled with laughter—until the paragons hushed them into reserved chuckles.

Amanda sprang back, appalled, mortified and without thinking. She wiped her hands clean on the skirt of her suit. Josh thought about breaking Jerry in half, but then Amanda wouldn't get her damn photo.

He caught her wrist and pulled her closer. "Ignore them."

"I'm...I'm done anyway." She tugged her wrist free and began tidying her hair, making sure no strands had escaped the elegant twist.

Used to be, Josh hated to see her fussing around. Wynn and Del seldom did the feminine fretting that seemed so much a part of Amanda.

But now that he understood Amanda better, he knew that she used the busy little movements to collect herself. His heart wrenched, seeing her look so lost, so alone.

Jerry appeared with a spray bottle and began misting him all over.

"Damn! *That's cold.*"

Jerry paid him no mind. "Almost done," he said, and then, "Close your eyes." He gave Josh just enough time to comply before spraying the oil right in his face.

"There. You're dirty, sweaty, everything a *real man* should be."

The irony in Jerry's tone couldn't be missed, and Josh shared his sentiments on that one.

Amanda protested. "It's not about being a real man. I just want the illusion that he's been hard at work. I want to capture the..." she cast about for a word, and settled on, "*drama* of fighting a fire."

This time Josh didn't take exception. He had a few troubling ideas about Amanda's preoccupation with the benefit calendar and her reluctance to get involved sexually. He hoped like hell he was wrong, and tonight he intended to find out. Whether his suspicions proved true or not, he still wanted her. More so every damn day.

But until then, he would treat her with kid gloves. "Let's get this over with," he said.

Amanda rushed to hand him his heavy ax. "Prop this on your shoulder, and lean on the tree."

"Prop it... What? Like Paul Bunyon?" he teased.

"No, like Josh Marshall, firefighter extraordinaire."

He shook his head, but inside he was pleased with her description. He sauntered to the tree, propped the ax handle on his shoulder and lifted his brows. "Good enough?"

"No." She rushed up close to him again. "You need a sexy smile."

Everyone else stood a respectable distance away—

Jerry adjusting his camera, Josh's friends huddled together by the car chuckling. Josh felt safe in touching her chin and saying, "I don't have anything to smile about right now."

"Bull. Your mind is probably crowded with thoughts of...physical things."

"My mind is crowded with thoughts of you."

She huffed. "Must you always be so difficult?"

"Yeah, because you're difficult." She drew up and he said quickly, "You know what would make me smile?"

"I'm afraid to ask."

Taking her by surprise, he leaned down and kissed her forehead. "Don't ever be afraid with me, okay?"

"I didn't mean... Okay, what? What does it take to make you smile?"

"Promise me a kiss."

Her eyes narrowed and her brows beetled. "You just took a kiss."

"Uh-uh. A real kiss. On the lips. Mouth open, a little tongue play..."

She started to turn away. Josh waited. She took half a step, crossed her arms around her middle, then propped her fists on her hips, then rubbed her temples. Such a telling reaction to such a small request!

Whirling back around to face him, Amanda asked in a low hiss, "Just what is it you hope to accomplish? I've told you I don't want to be involved."

"Even to a teenager," he explained gently, "one kiss doesn't equal involvement."

"But if I kiss you once..." Her voice tapered off like a fading echo.

"What?" Damn he wanted to touch her. He wished like hell that they were already alone. "You might want to kiss me again?"

Sounding tortured, she said, "Yes."

It felt like his knees got knocked out from under him. "Ah, babe..."

Jerry yelled, "Ready when you two are."

Josh touched the small gold hoop in her left ear. "Promise me, Amanda. Give me something sexy to think about, a reason to smile."

She closed her eyes, swallowed hard. "Okay."

The sexy little smile came of its own accord. So did the boner, but damn, he'd never in his life anticipated a kiss quite so much.

Luckily, the bunker pants were, by necessity, thick and insulated. It'd take an impressive man indeed to tent them.

Amanda looked at him, her eyes widened, and she quickly backed up. "There, Jerry! Take that shot."

Josh continued to watch her, their gazes locked and his imagination in overdrive, while Amanda backed away and Jerry's camera clicked enthusiastically.

Amanda blushed, her brown eyes darkened, her lips parted. Josh took it all in, all the signs of beginning arousal, and wanted to groan. He knew his own face was flushed and his eyes hot, but it was so much like foreplay, sharing thoughts with her this way.

Amanda kept backing up until she was eventually

pressed to a wide bare tree trunk. Her arms were crossed over her middle and her chest rose and fell with her breaths. Josh thought about taking her right there in the woods, with the cool air around them, his hands protecting her soft bottom from the rough bark, lifting her, grinding her forward...

But Amanda, with her prissy suits and polished appearance, likely wouldn't appreciate a romp in the dirt.

He'd have to be patient—not his strong suit.

"All done," Jerry called out. "I think I got some good ones. I don't know what you said to him, Ms. Barker, but..."

"Nothing! I didn't say anything to him!"

"Then he's one hell of an actor." Jerry, not one for small talk, saluted them both and headed back to his car.

Josh called out, "When will the prints be ready?"

"It's a rush job," Jerry answered. "I can pull them up on the computer tonight. Amanda can have the disk to look over tomorrow morning. Once she chooses which shots she wants I can have 'em ready in a day."

Amanda, still looking tongue-tied, pushed herself away from the tree and rushed after Jerry. Josh approached Mick and Zack.

Without preamble, he said to both men, "Take off, will you?"

Mick grinned. "You got plans?"

Del elbowed her husband. "Of course he does. Did you see the way they were looking at each other?"

Zack edged in. "What happened with that business of her not wanting you?"

Wynn pretended to reel. "My God! You mean there's a woman who doesn't want Josh?" She shook her head, making her frizzy hair bounce. "No. I refuse to believe it. All my illusions will be destroyed."

Zack pinched her behind, and she jumped.

Laughing under his breath, Josh said, "Yeah, a few actually." He gave Wynn and Del pointed looks, because they had indeed made their sincere disinterest well known. Then he explained, "I don't know what's going on, but I hope to find out. Only I can't find out a thing with the curious quartet hanging around, watching my every move."

Zack leaned around his wife to see Mick. "Does he mean us?"

Mick nodded slowly. "I think he might."

Del swatted her husband, then went on tiptoe to kiss Josh's cheek. "We'll drag them away. And good luck."

"Careful," Zack told his wife when she went to kiss Josh, too. "You'll get all greasy."

Wynn was tall enough that she could reach Josh's cheek without bracing on him anywhere. "You'll win her over with your charm," she assured him, all kidding put aside.

Josh remembered a day when Wynn hadn't noticed

his charm, but evidently she considered her resistance superior to that of most women.

Half a second later Amanda was at his side, scowling, furious maybe. Her normally arched brows were lowered in a dark frown and her mouth looked pinched. "What's going on here? Why is everyone kissing you?"

"Just saying goodbye," Mick told her, and he and Del turned to get in the car.

Zack said, "I hope you got some good shots, Ms. Barker. Thanks for letting us observe." And he and Wynn also got into the car.

Amanda just stood there, looking self-conscious and bemused. Together they watched the car back out and drive away, Jerry following close behind them.

Josh looked down at her, and said softly, "Alone at last."

She blinked several times, her nervousness so apparent that Josh wanted to just lift her and hold her and rock her in his arms. Instead, he caught her chin on the edge of his hand.

His heart thundered, surprising him with his over-the-top response. Amanda breathed hard, her hands fluttered, then settled on the waistband of the heavy pants, just over where his suspenders connected in the front.

He leaned down, touched his mouth to hers, heard her soft moan, and like a virgin on prom night, he lost it.

# 5

AMANDA'S HANDS slid over Josh's oiled shoulders, up to his neck where she caught him and held on tight. Josh forgot about her nice gray suit and matching cape, about her styled hair and her reservations.

All his senses were focused on the fact of her kissing him, her taste, her indescribable scent, the feeling of rightness having her small body inching closer and closer to his own.

He tunneled his fingers through her hair, dislodging pins and clips to cradle her skull, to keep her mouth under his so he could continue to kiss her. Her mouth was hot and sweet and her tongue shyly touched his own.

Her breasts, discreetly covered by bra and blouse, suit and cape, brushed his abdomen with the impact of a thunderclap. Josh tilted his pelvis into her, lifted her to her toes, crushed her close.

She was such a petite woman, all softness and sweetness and femininity. She took his breath away with the need to devour her, the urge to protect her.

She bit his bottom lip and her nails sank into his shoulders. Slowly, in small degrees, Josh lifted his mouth. "Baby, you burn me up."

Her beautiful brown eyes, heavy and unfocused, stared at his mouth. She licked the corner of her lips and whispered, *"Yes."*

Josh groaned and kissed her again. He didn't know how long it had been for her, but he felt like he hadn't had sex in years and now he was at the boiling point. Even through the damn bunker pants, he was aware of Amanda's pelvis pressing into his swollen erection with blatant, yet probably unconscious, invitation.

Her cape was soft—and easily removed. Amanda didn't even seem to notice when it fluttered to the ground to land around their feet in a soft gray heap of material.

He slid his hand down her back, over her curvy hip to the bottom of her sweet cheek. He groaned low in his throat—damn, but she had a nice ass, firm and round.

He hadn't realized. Her suits did a lot of concealing, not that he minded. The last thing he wanted was every other guy ogling her butt. Or for that matter any part of her anatomy.

Edging his hand farther downward, he found the hem of her skirt and tugged it up enough to let his fingers drift over her nylon-covered thigh. Her breath hitched as he went higher and higher...when he reached the edge of a garter, he nearly collapsed.

"You little sneak," he murmured, his mouth still touching hers, but gently now. His fingertips encountered the warm, bare satiny flesh at the back of her thigh and he stroked her. "You came here today with sexy stockings, and you weren't even going to tell me."

Amanda went still, then she stumbled out of his arms so quickly she tripped over the cape and landed on her rump. Josh tried to catch her, but he wasn't quick enough. She'd taken him totally by surprise and now she was sprawled at his feet, staring up at him in horror, her face utterly white.

She'd landed more on the cape than off it. She had one hand braced on a clump of dirt, the other pushing frantically at the hem of her skirt. Her knees were pressed together, her feet apart, giving her an adorably posed look, especially in the high heels and prim suit, her hair more down than up, her lipstick now gone.

Josh felt hornier than ever, and more confused.

He knelt down in front of her, elbows braced on his knees, his hands dangling, hoping to appear relaxed when he was so tense a touch could shatter him. "What is it, sweetheart?"

She scampered back, her heels kicking up the hard ground and her skirt rising a little more, showing a sexy stretch of slim smooth thigh and the edge of a lacy garter. Damn she had nice legs. Before she could go entirely out of his reach, Josh caught her left ankle.

"Hold up. I just want to know what's wrong."

She started to smooth her suit jacket with busy hands, realized it was now covered in the baby oil that coated his chest and she grimaced. "My suit is ruined."

"I'll buy you another one."

Her head flashed up so quickly, she startled him. "You will not!"

"I ruined it," he pointed out reasonably, still with his long fingers wrapped around her ankle.

"You did no such thing. It was...it was me and my behavior..."

"We kissed, Amanda. There was no behavior, at least not the way you're saying it, as if you killed someone."

Her eyes widened and she gasped. Just as quickly, she turned her head to stare toward the woods. "Josh please, let me go."

"Hell, no. Not until you explain."

"You have to be cold!"

"Not even close." She looked disbelieving and he shook his head. "Nice try, but after the way you kissed me, you gotta know I'm burning up."

Amanda pulled herself together. It was a visible effort, and Josh watched in fascination—and remorse— as her cold shell fell into place. "I told you this wasn't what I wanted. But as you just said, you got your kiss. So now we're through."

Josh thought about his options, letting them run through his mind in rapid order, sorting and picking until he decided on the only course of action that just might get him what he wanted—her trust. And ultimately, her.

Maintaining his hold on her ankle, he levered himself over her, moving slowly to cover her, not letting her draw away.

"Josh!"

"Shh," he soothed. "I just want to talk and we can't say anything important when all you want to do is lock me out."

"We're in a public park!"

Raised on one elbow, she flattened a hand on his chest to ward him off. Josh released her ankle and caught her shoulders, then pressed her down to lie flat. "No one is around."

She turned her head so far to the side her nose touched the ground. "I don't want you to do this," she said in a voice gone thin and shrill.

"Oh? Is that why your pulse is racing?" He kissed the tiny telltale fluttering of excitement in her throat. "Besides, I'm not going to do anything to you. At least know that much, Amanda. I'd never force you."

She squeezed her eyes shut, and said, "I know it."

That was something, he supposed. Not much, but it'd have to do for now. "Amanda? Come on, look at me, honey." He knew she wouldn't so he cupped her head and brought her face around to his. "I want to ask you a few things, and I want you to know that no matter the answer, it won't make a difference about how I feel."

Her lips, swollen from his kisses, parted. "How do you feel?"

With a tiny smile he couldn't contain, Josh admitted, "Poleaxed. Dumbfounded. Smitten, bit, infatuated and so physically attracted I'm learning to live with a perpetual hard-on."

Her eyes grew round, her pupils dilated. "For me?"

Now he laughed out loud. He kissed the end of her nose and said, "Yeah, for you. And it isn't easy being here with you like this, on top of you, able to smell you—"

She scoffed. "There you go with the smell thing again."

He nuzzled his nose against her cheek and whispered in a voice gone husky, "I love how you smell."

Her lashes fluttered at the *L* word, and again she turned her head to the side.

"Amanda," he chided. "Don't hide from me."

She nodded, looked at him directly, and whispered, "Thank you."

"You're welcome." Josh wasn't at all sure what she thanked him for, and at the moment, he didn't care. He prepared himself and blurted, "Were you burned?"

Her whole body stiffened and jerked. The word, *"No,"* exploded from her and she began to struggle. "I wasn't," she said, still fighting. *"I wasn't."*

"Amanda, I swear it doesn't matter to me!" Josh easily subdued her, catching her wrists and pinning them beside her head. His own throat felt tight, making it hard to speak, even harder to breathe. Her legs shifted under his but he was so much bigger, she had no way to dislodge him. "It doesn't matter, honey. If you have scars..."

"No!" She shook her head hard, ruining her hair and bumping his chin. "I was never burned. You don't understand..."

She practically sobbed out those words and Josh, his heart breaking but needing to know, said, "Then explain it to me. Make me understand."

She stopped fighting him to press against him. He was so stunned he released her arms and she flung them around his neck, squeezing him so tight he felt it in his heart, in his soul. Her hot, frantic breaths pelted his throat and the wetness of her tears touched his shoulder.

He squeezed his own eyes shut. "Amanda?"

"I wasn't burned," she swore with raw guilt, her voice shuddering, her body shaking. "I wasn't even in the fire."

*The fire.* Discovering he was right, that there had in fact been a fire gave Josh no satisfaction. Instead, it made his skin crawl and his stomach cramp with thoughts of what she might have gone through. He knew firsthand the damage a blaze could cause, both physically and emotionally.

At least Amanda claimed she hadn't been in the fire, not that it would matter to him now if she had been burned. He'd meant what he said. But then what *had* happened?

Josh knew he had to go slowly. Cradling Amanda

close, keeping her tucked protectively to his chest, he sat up. He brought her into his lap and just held her.

Someone she loved had been burned? Another man? Questions raced through his mind, but he didn't dare push her. She was already at the end of her rope, and he knew how she'd feel once she regained control. She'd blame him, and he'd have to start over from scratch.

Josh nuzzled her cheek, seeking forgiveness, because despite what he'd just told himself, he needed to know.

Hoping to help soothe her, he coasted his hands up and down her narrow back and kept on kissing her, her temple, her hair, her ear. He didn't care where, so long as he got to kiss her.

Minutes slipped by and neither of them broke the quiet. The sun sank down behind the bare, gnarled treetops, leaving the park shadowed and cold. A breeze rustled the dry grasses and brush, chilling his naked upper body.

Sounding sleepy, Amanda rubbed her fingers over his chest and muttered, "You're all slippery."

He smiled. That wasn't at all what he'd expected to hear from her after her emotional display and the lengthy silence.

She lifted her face and he saw her cheek was shiny with tears and baby oil. Around her right eye the blackening made her look wounded, bruised. A thin smear decorated her chin, the fine line of her delicate jaw, the edge of her nose.

It seemed the rightest thing in the world to lean down and kiss her mouth.

She kissed him back, letting the touch of their mouths linger, long and soft and caring.

"I'm sorry," she said on a sigh, snuggling close again, unmindful of the mess their embrace had already caused to her appearance. "I don't usually carry on like a deranged woman."

"Not deranged," Josh corrected. "Upset. We all get upset sometimes. It's nothing to apologize for."

Amanda nodded and then started to rise. His arms tightened. "Hey," he asked gently, "where do you think you're going?"

"Just to get your shirt. I don't want you to catch a cold and it's getting nippy."

True. Chills roughened Josh's skin and made him shiver. Still, he didn't want to move. With Amanda in his lap, he felt more content than he had in weeks. But because he'd been forward enough for her to bring sexual assault charges against him, he helped her to stand.

She tottered for a moment, her legs unsteady as she looked around to locate his discarded clothes on the picnic table. Her steps methodical, a bit too slow, Amanda fetched the jeans and his T-shirt and flannel.

Josh rose, too, brushing off his backside and wishing he could read her mind. With most women, his confidence was iron strong, but Amanda was an enigma and he never knew for sure where he stood with her.

He watched her lift his flannel to her nose and inhale for just a second, before crushing it close and strolling back to him.

"Here," she said, acting as if nothing had happened, as if she hadn't just lost control in front of him.

As if she hadn't kissed him to the point of no return—and then backed down.

Josh accepted the clothes and yanked his shirt on over his head. It stuck to him, thanks to the oil and blackening. As a fireman, he'd had many occasions where soot had coated his body, even getting beneath his gloves to cake under his nails. By comparison, a little oil could be ignored.

He shrugged the flannel on while Amanda watched, her expression distant, impossible to read.

"If you don't mind," Josh said, "I'll change pants, too. These aren't exactly the best to drive in."

"All right." She bent to get her cape. Dried leaves and twigs stuck to the material so she shook it out, then gave him her back.

Josh noticed a run in one of her stockings, dirt on her dressy high-heeled shoes, blackening and oil streaks on her once-impeccable clothing.

He felt like a marauder, like a ravisher of innocents. But damn it, he didn't know how to deal with her. It was like floundering in the dark. He had to push her, or give up on her, and giving her up wasn't an option.

Her back still to him, Amanda put her fingers to her hair and discovered how he'd wrecked it with his impatient hands. Personally, Josh thought she looked sexy as hell rumpled—even with the grease streaks on her face—but he knew she wouldn't agree.

He watched Amanda as she fussed with her hair for a few moments, then her head dropped forward when she realized there was no way to repair it, not out in the park near the woods with only the diminishing sunset and a tugging breeze to help her.

One by one, she began removing pins, and with each silky light-brown lock that fell over her shoulders, Josh's heart punched hard. He skinned out of his bunker gear and steel-toed boots, and tugged on his jeans, awkwardly hopping on first one foot then the other while keeping his attention on Amanda. He stepped into his shoes, slipped his thick leather belt through the loops and bundled up the rest of his gear.

By that time, Amanda's long hair was free and she combed her fingers through it, trying to bring some order to the tumbled mass. Her movements were innocently seductive and sexual. Unable to stand the physical and emotional distance between them, Josh approached her.

He clasped her shoulders. "Amanda, are you ready to talk now?"

She reached back and patted his hand in a distracted, almost avuncular way. "Why don't we talk in the car?" Even as she asked that, the wind picked up, tossing her hair so that the silky strands brushed his chin and throat.

He shuddered with raw need.

Amanda shivered with cold.

The park was dark now, cast in long eerie shadows. Josh hadn't realized how quickly the sun would set once it began its decline. But with the tall trees surrounding them, little of the fading light could penetrate.

He didn't want to leave, but then he was aroused and equally concerned. With the odd combination of emotions, he knew he wasn't thinking straight.

"You're cold," he said, giving himself a reason to stroke her, to rub his hands up and down her arms under the guise of warming her. What he really wanted to do with her and to her would no doubt make her hotter than hell. It was certainly making him hot just thinking about it. But for now, he had to content himself with a little arm rubbing.

Amanda patted his hand again, then turned to face him. "I just think it's best if we get on our way."

Her eyes looked luminous in the dark, her skin pale.

"You're not afraid of me?"

She shook her head. "No."

"You're going to talk to me, to help me understand?"

"Yes. I'll try."

Josh searched her face, trying to read the truth there, but Amanda always did a good job of closing down on him whenever she wanted to. He tucked his extra clothes under his arm and hefted the ax. "Let's go."

Once they were in the car she said, "I still need you to sign the release."

"Sure." He started the car, flipped on the headlights, and drove out. "As soon as I approve the pictures you'll be using."

Her sound of impatience turned into a laugh. "You are so impossible, Josh Marshall. What am I going to do with you?"

*Love me.* The wayward thought scared the hell out of him, making his hands tighten on the wheel, his heart pound, his stomach roil and his brain stutter. He'd never before wanted a woman to really care.

His throat burned with the need to curse, to rage at the fickle hand of fate that had shown him a woman he wanted more than any other, only to keep her out of reach because she didn't feel the same.

After so many women had admired him, women who were attracted to him, some of them a little in love with him, he was deathly afraid he'd gone and stupidly fallen for Amanda.

"Talk to me," he said. "That's what you can do."

"All right." She seemed very small and still in the car beside him. Her tone was hesitant, but she continued. "First, the reason I don't want to get involved with you is that there's no point. Beyond what we just did, things can't progress."

Having no idea what she was trying to say, he asked only, "Why not?"

"I'm not...capable of it."

He swung his head toward her, then forced himself to watch the road. *Not capable, not capable, not capable...*

"I'm a little slow here, babe. Can you explain that?"

"Quit calling me babe and I might try."

He shook his head. Damn, she could make him nuts. "Go ahead."

"I'm twenty-four years old, Josh."

"So? I figured you to be somewhere around there. I'm twenty-seven."

"I've never been intimate with a man. I'm still a...a virgin."

His heart lurched. Before his sluggish brain could assimilate that confession and make sense of it, she continued.

"That's not by choice. I tried a few times, but..."

Her voice turned cold, remote. It was as if she'd gone on automatic pilot, telling him things he'd insisted on hearing, but not allowing them to hurt her again.

Josh blindly reached for her hand. It didn't matter whether or not she needed the touch, because *he* needed it.

"Sometimes stuff happens in our lives and it affects us. When I was younger I did some really horrible things."

"Just a second here, okay?" He tried to keep his tone reassuring. "Are we talking physical reasons why you can't, or emotional reasons?"

She laughed. "I've got all the same parts as any

other woman, they just don't work right. And the doctors call it mental, not emotional."

"I don't give a rat's ass what they call it."

She squeezed his fingers. "It's all right. I've accepted my life."

"Well good for you, but I'm not accepting it." He'd be damned before he'd accept this as anything other than an emotional setback. "And you're only giving me bits and pieces of stuff here. Amanda, I *care* about you."

Her next words were choked. "I'm sorry. I wish you didn't. I don't want to hurt anyone ever again. Not for the rest of my life." She dug in her purse for a tissue and blew her nose. After a shuddering breath that ripped out his heart, she said, "All I want to do now is try to make up for things in the only way I can."

"The calendar?" he asked.

"Yes. And other projects, other ways to help those who've been hurt or killed. Some things, well, there's no way to make up for them. They happen and you have to live with the consequences."

It was a good thing, to Josh's way of thinking, that her home wasn't far from the park. Otherwise, he'd have pulled over on the side of the road. But he reached her driveway and rather than stop at the end as he was sure she'd prefer, he drove right up to the front walkway.

Then he sat there in stunned disbelief as his headlights landed on the front and side of her home. Would Amanda just keep knocking him off balance?

"Is this a schoolhouse?" he asked.

"It used to be, yes."

The tiny rectangular building of aged red brick had two arched windows on each outer wall and an arched double front door of thick planked wood. The steep roof had slate shingles and a small chimney protruded off the backside. It looked like a fairy cottage, set in the middle of towering trees and scraggly lawn with dead ivy climbing up the brick here and there, waving out like a lady's hair caught in the breeze.

Other than the driveway that ended at the side of the house where he could see her Beetle parked under a shelter, and a short path to the front door, there was no relief from those tall oaks and elms and evergreens. No neighbors, no traffic, no real lawn to speak of, no...nothing.

She'd isolated herself so thoroughly that Josh wanted to get out and howl at the moon.

He wanted to take her back to his place where it was noisy and busy with life.

He wanted to keep her.

Amanda opened her car door and stepped out. Josh followed, fearful that she'd skip away from him and he'd never get his answers. No way in hell could he sleep tonight with only half the story, and her hanging confession about virginity.

Looking at her over the hood of the Firebird, he said, "Ask me in."

She tipped her head back and looked up at the tree-tops, swaying against a dark gray sky. "I suppose I might as well," she said with little enthusiasm. "We can finish this, and you can sign the release and it'll be done."

So saying, she found her key in her purse and walked on a short cobblestone path to the front door. Josh listened to the hollow echoing of her high heels on the rounded stone.

*Finish it? Ha! Not by a long shot.*

Tonight, to his way of thinking, was just the beginning.

AMANDA WATCHED as Josh stepped into her quaint little eclectic home. She flipped on a wall switch, which lit a tiny side-table candle lamp. While he stood in the doorframe, she went on through the minuscule family room and into the kitchen to turn on the brighter fluorescent overhead lights. Whenever she needed light to work by, she used the two-seat kitchenette table. Even now, it was filled with photos and contracts for the calendar.

Her home was barely big enough for one, and with Josh inside, it was most definitely crowded. Especially when he closed the door. He looked around with a sense of wonder, then said the most unexpected thing.

"I thought you were rich."

After all the emotional upheaval, Amanda burst out laughing. She peered at Josh, saw his look of chagrin, and laughed some more.

His expression changed and he stalked toward her. "I do love it when you laugh." She stalled, realization of their situation sinking in, and he said, "I also thought you'd be immaculate."

Shrugging, Amanda looked around at the clutter. "No time. I work a regular forty-hour week like most people, then put in another twenty hours or more a week on projects. My place is never really dirty, but yes, it's usually messy."

Dishes filled the small sink and an overloaded laundry hamper sat on the floor. Amanda shrugged again. She did what she could, when she could. If Josh didn't like it, he shouldn't have invited himself in.

"I wasn't complaining," he said. "It just surprised me. Will you show me the rest of your place?"

Amanda gathered herself. She'd explain things to him, but there was no reason for more hysterics, no reason for an excess of the pitiful, useless tears and dramatics fit for the stage.

What had happened to her was the least tragic thing that had occurred that awful night. She wouldn't allow herself to pretend otherwise.

"There's not much to show, only the four rooms. You've already seen two of them, the family room and kitchen."

"No television," he noted.

"It's in my bedroom, along with a stereo, through here." The house measured a mere fifty feet by thirty feet. The front double doors were centered on the overall width of the house, which put them into the far left of the family room. An open archway, draped with gauzy swag curtains in lieu of a door, showed her bedroom. The curtains weren't adequate for privacy, but since she lived alone, it had never mattered.

Straight ahead of the family room was the kitchen. The two rooms seemed to meld together, with only the side of the refrigerator and the location of her tiny table to serve as a divider.

The kitchen was just large enough for a stacking washer and dryer, a parlor table, an apartment-size stove and her refrigerator. The cabinets were almost nonexistent, but open shelving and one pantry offered her all the storage space she needed.

At the back of the house, opposite the kitchen, was the minuscule bathroom that opened both into her bedroom and into the kitchen.

A bare toilet, a pedestal sink and a claw-foot tub filled the room with elegant simplicity. Other than the creamy ceramic tile in the bathroom, the whole house had original rich wood flooring.

Josh peeked into each room. Her bedroom had a full-size cherry bed and one nightstand that held an alarm clock, phone and lamp. A large ornate armoire held her clothes and a TV-VCR combination. Her modest stereo sat on the floor beside it.

One narrow dim closet was situated next to the

door for the bathroom. It wasn't deep enough to accommodate hangers, so she had installed shelves and stored her shoes and slacks and sweaters there.

The tall, wide windows and cathedral ceilings made the house look larger than it was. The absence of doors gave it a fresh openness, while natural wood furniture and earth tone materials brought everything together.

"I like it," Josh said, and she could see that he did. His eyes practically glowed when he stared at her old-fashioned bathtub. "How old is this place?"

"An engraved stone plaque, embedded above the front door, says it was erected in 1905. I had to do some work to it before I could live here. Some of the windowpanes were busted out and the roof leaked. The floors all had to be sanded and repaired."

Hands on his hips, Josh looked around again and shook his head. "A schoolhouse."

"A hunter had converted it into a cottage years ago. He's the one who put in modern plumbing and electricity. When he passed away, his kids just sort of forgot about it for a long, long time. I'm glad they finally decided to sell because I love it."

"Lots of charm," Josh agreed. "You know, you need a school bell."

"I have one. It's in the back, next to the well."

"A bona fide well?"

"Yes." She smiled at his enthusiasm over that bit of whimsy. "It even works, though I can't bring myself to drink anything out of it. I guess I'm too used to tap water."

They still stood in her bedroom, and Amanda began to feel a little uncomfortable. "Should I make some coffee? Not that I think this will take long, but..." She headed out of the room, assuming Josh would follow.

Of course, he didn't. "I'd rather talk."

"Fine." She clasped her hands together. "Let's at least sit down."

Josh nodded and followed her into the family room. She had only enough room for one bookshelf, a loveseat with end tables and lamps and a rocking chair. Josh tugged her down into the loveseat, and then kept hold of her hand.

"So you're a virgin?" he asked in that bald, shocking way of his. "That's not a crime, you know. Especially these days."

Many times in her life, Amanda had forced herself to face her accusers, to face the truth while trying to apologize, to make amends even when she knew that to be impossible.

She could force herself to face Josh, and to tell him the whole story. "I told you it's not a moral choice. I tried, several times, but I'm frigid."

He lifted his free hand to stroke her hair, and ended up removing a piece of a twig. He smiled at it while saying, "You didn't seem frigid to me. Just the opposite."

Her reaction to Josh had surprised her, too, but she

wouldn't be fooled. Too many times she had thought herself whole—perhaps forgiven—only to be disappointed again.

Shaking her head, Amanda said, "I want what you want, that's not the problem. But you saw what happened. I can only go so far and then I start remembering and then I...I just can't."

"What?" Josh cupped her chin and brought her face around to his. "What do you remember?"

"Josh...are you sure you want to hear this?" She felt she had to give him one last chance to leave without causing an unpleasant scene. It'd be easier for both of them. "You could just let it go," she suggested, "just sign the release and leave."

"I'm not going anywhere, so quit stalling. And quit acting like whatever you have to tell me will horrify me and send me racing out the door. That won't happen, Amanda."

He twisted further in his seat to hold her shoulders and give her a gentle shake. "When I said I cared about you, I meant it. I don't go around saying that to every woman I want to have sex with."

She laughed. He was so outrageously honest about his intentions.

Josh wasn't amused. "When I said scars wouldn't matter, I meant that, too. It doesn't make any difference to me if the scars are on your body or in your heart. They're still a part of you, and so I want to know. All of it."

Well she'd tried. If it took the full truth to make him

understand, then she'd give him the full truth. Amanda looked him in the eyes and said, "When I was seventeen, I killed a man."

Josh froze, his expression arrested, disbelieving.

Better to get it all over with quickly, she thought. "I also wounded two others. They're the ones who wear the awful scars, not me. God knows it would have been so much better, and certainly more just, if it had been me. But that's not how it worked out."

"Amanda..."

She shook her head. "There are so many people who will never forgive me, but that's okay, because I won't ever forgive myself."

# 6

JOSH SHOCKED the breath right out of her when he yanked her into his arms. He felt so solid, so strong and brave and heroic. He was everything she could never be.

It seemed criminal for her to be with him, but Amanda couldn't stop herself from knotting her hands in his T-shirt and clinging to him.

He sat back and again lifted her into his lap. In a voice gone hoarse with emotion, he said, "Tell me what happened."

That he bothered to ask for details amazed Amanda. A few men had, men she'd tried and failed to be intimate with in college, and when she'd first moved here. But macabre fascination and selfish intent had motivated their queries, because they wanted to know why they were being rejected. Not one of them had asked out of genuine caring.

She *felt* Josh's caring. She felt it in the way he held her, in the steady drone of his heartbeat against her cheek, in the way his large hands moved up and down her spine, offering her comfort. It settled over her like a warm blanket, almost tangible.

Tears pricked her eyes, but she staved them off.

She'd cried enough, and besides, she didn't deserve to sit around whining.

Amanda rubbed her cheek against him, breathing in his masculine scent. "You were right—I did come from money. Dad not only has his own company and more stock in other companies than I can remember, but he inherited a fortune from his family. My mother's family isn't quite as well off, but they're definitely upper-crust. Whenever they weren't around, there was a housekeeper or tutor or someone to keep tabs on me and my sister."

"You said you were seventeen? That's a little old to have a baby-sitter, isn't it?"

"I thought so. But my parents were determined that my sister and I would never embarrass them. So many of their friends had kids who had gotten into trouble, unwanted pregnancies, drugs, bad grades. I don't blame them for being extra cautious. Being influential puts you in the limelight, so we had be exemplary in every way."

"Sounds rough."

She started to lift her head, but he pressed her back down and kissed her temple. She subsided. "Don't get me wrong, my parents loved me."

"*Loved* you? As in past tense?"

She didn't want to delve too deeply into the broken ties with her family. It hurt too much. "Things have been...strained since that awful night. I embarrassed them. I caused a huge scandal that still hasn't died down, even though it happened seven years ago. We keep in touch, but I doubt we'll ever be close again."

"Tell me what happened."

Deciding to just get it over with, she said, "One night I slipped out of my house to meet with my boyfriend. We were going to have sex in the woods behind my house. Can you believe that? A very risqué, exciting rendezvous. I felt totally wicked and very grown-up." She lowered her head and laughed though she'd never remember that night with anything but horror. "Looking back, I realize how immature and ridiculous I was."

"You were young," Josh said without censure, "and most seventeen-year-olds are ready to start experimenting, to start pushing for independence. You sound pretty average to me."

If she had ever been average, Amanda thought, she'd been changed that awful night. "He showed up at midnight. I crawled out my second-story bedroom window and shimmied down a tree, and away we went." She absently plucked at a wrinkle in her skirt, not seeing anything, not wanting to see. "While I was gone, making out in the dirt on a borrowed blanket, our house caught on fire. An electrical short or something they eventually decided. Everyone got out of the house by the time the fire trucks arrived, only..."

The muscles in Josh's arms bunched. He was a firefighter, so she knew he could easily picture the scenario. "Only when no one found you, they all thought you were still inside?"

"Yes." She swallowed hard, but the lump of regret remained. "My parents were hysterical. My mother collapsed on the lawn with my sister, both of them screaming. My father tried to get back inside when he couldn't find me. He punched two firefighters who tried to hold him back, but he finally gave up when three of them went inside instead."

Remorse clawed through her, as fresh and painful as the day it had happened. "My bedroom was in the middle of the upstairs floor. While they were searching for me, going on my parents' assurances that I had to be in there, the floor caved in. One man..." An invisible fist squeezed her throat, choking her. God, she hated reliving that awful night.

Josh waited, not saying a word, just stroking her.

"Even in the woods, I heard the sirens. They seemed to be right on top of us and I was afraid they'd wake my family and they'd know what I did, that I'd sneaked out. So I came home."

Shuddering, rubbing at her eyes so she could see, Amanda said, "The fireman fell into the downstairs and got trapped. He was unconscious and the smoke was so thick, they almost couldn't find him. By the time they got him out he was badly burned."

She gave up trying to wipe away the tears and just dropped her hands into her lap. "He only lived three days. Three days of wavering in and out of consciousness, constantly in pain."

Josh still didn't say anything, but there was such a ringing in her head she wouldn't have heard him anyway. She tried to breathe but couldn't. She tried to relax, to be unemotional, but she couldn't do that either. "The other two men are badly scarred, their arms, and their hands."

Pushing herself away from Josh's embrace, she rocked forward and covered her face, ashamed and embarrassed and sick at heart. "They hated me of course. Not that I blame them. And that man's widow..."

She felt Josh touch her shoulder and she lurched to her feet, then paced to the window. She couldn't talk anymore, but there wasn't much else to say. She stared blindly out at the blackness of her yard, and the blackness of her life.

Then Josh was behind her, drawing her into his warmth, wrapping those incredibly strong arms around her so she had no choice but to give him his way.

"Hush now," he said.

Amanda felt her mascara run, knew she needed to blow her nose. "It was on the news," she said, the words coming on their own. "My parents screaming, the firefighters working so hard, dirty and beat but not giving up. They had videos of my mother in her nightgown, curlers in her hair, my sister bawling. And my father, such a stately, dignified man...acting almost insane, fighting the firemen."

"Trying to get to the daughter he loves. That's typical, Amanda."

"They showed the videos of me, too, just standing

there, not hurt, not even in the house. My hair was wrecked, a tangled mess, and my blouse was buttoned wrong. There were weeds on my clothes and...everyone knew. They knew where I'd been and what I'd been doing and my parents were just devastated." She squeezed herself tight, but it didn't help. "It wasn't only on the local news, it was on every station everywhere."

Josh turned her.

She couldn't look at him yet so she pushed away and went to the table for a tissue, blowing her nose loudly and then hiccuping. When she did finally look at Josh, she saw his pity, his sad eyes, and she wanted to die.

"My dad took me to the hospital to see the two men who survived." The things she'd seen that night would live with her forever. There were still nights when she couldn't sleep, when she'd close her eyes and relive every frightening, too real moment. "It was so awful. Firemen pacing, wives crying, and they all looked at me like I'd done it on purpose."

"No," Josh said quietly. "I can't believe that."

Memories bombarded her, and she said, "You're right." Amanda recalled an incredible incident. "One of the firemen who'd gone inside for me, Marcus Lindsey, told me he had a daughter my age. He told me kids made mistakes and that he didn't blame me, so he didn't want me blaming myself. He told me I was too pretty to keep crying."

A new wash of tears came with that admission.

Marcus Lindsey was an unbelievable man, a hero, like most firefighters. He'd deserved so much better than what had happened because of her.

Josh touched her hair. "And he's right. We know the risks inherent in our jobs. Lindsey did what he's supposed to do."

"He spent weeks in the hospital, and he'll carry the scars for the rest of his life. He's not a fireman anymore. Neither of the survivors are." She blinked and more tears rolled down her cheeks.

Josh plucked another tissue and wiped her face. He was so gentle and tender it amazed Amanda. "What happened was a freak accident," he murmured, "not a deliberate act, definitely not something to keep beating yourself up for."

Amanda couldn't believe his reaction. "How would you feel? If you'd done what I did, if you'd slipped off against your parents' instruction to fool around in the woods and someone had *died* because of it, how would you feel?"

"There's no way I can answer that, honey, because it didn't happen to me." He tucked her hair behind her ear, rubbed her temple with his thumb. "But I can tell you that I've made mistakes, in my job and in my social life. Everybody has—it's one of the side effects of being human. All we can do is try not to make the same mistakes again, to forgive ourselves, and to make amends."

"I'm trying to make amends."

"No, you're driving yourself into the ground with guilt. It's not at all the same thing."

Confusion swamped her. He sounded so reasonable, when there was nothing reasonable about what had happened.

"Tell you what," Josh said. "Why don't you go take a warm shower? Your clothes are dirty and torn and your makeup is everywhere it's not supposed to be."

"Oh." She started to touch her face, but he caught her hands and kissed her forehead.

"You look like a very adorable urchin, so don't worry about it. But I know you'll be more comfortable if you shower and change. While you do that I'll go ahead and make some coffee. Are you hungry? I could maybe rustle you up a sandwich."

Amanda pushed her hair out of her face and looked around her small house in consternation. She'd bared her soul, then prepared for the worst. But not only wasn't Josh disgusted, he offered to fix her food.

He could muddle her so easily. "You plan to make yourself at home in my kitchen?"

"Yes."

Truth was, Amanda didn't want him to leave. She felt spent, wasted right down to the bone, and she didn't want to be alone. He wasn't blaming her, wasn't appalled or shocked or disapproving. He'd listened and offered comfort.

It was so much more than she usually got, so much more than she thought she deserved.

She was selfish enough to want him to stay.

And realistic enough to know it wouldn't make a difference in the long run.

"All right, but no food. I'm not hungry."

Josh gave her a long look. "Can you manage on your own?"

"To shower?" She frowned. "Of course I can."

"Spoilsport."

Amanda stared. Now he wanted to tease her?

Smiling, Josh bent and kissed her softly on the mouth. "I'll be in the kitchen waiting."

Amanda watched Josh stroll from the room, a tall powerful man who had invaded her heart and then her home. Despite what she'd just confessed, he appeared to have no intention of withdrawing.

Amazing. From the start, Josh had seen the worst from her. She'd been first badgering and defensive to gain his involvement in the calendar, then hysterical and tearful while giving him her truths. He knew all her worst qualities and her darkest secret, yet he didn't leave.

From deep, deep in her heart, something warm and happy and unfamiliar stirred.

It scared her spitless, because what would happen when he realized their relationship would never be an intimate one? Would he remain her friend? Somehow, she doubted it. Josh was a very physical, a very sexual man.

That meant that she had to take advantage of every single second she'd have with him.

Amanda hurried to get through with her shower.

JOSH WAITED until he heard the pipes rumble from her shower, then he punched the wall, hurting his knuckles but relieving some of his anger. Luckily, the old schoolhouse was solid so all he hurt was himself.

He couldn't remember ever being so enraged, to the point he'd have gladly horsewhipped a few people, starting with himself. Everything that had happened since first meeting her now had fresh meaning. And it hurt.

He wanted to pass backward in time and save a young lady from a life-altering mistake.

He wanted to redo about a hundred moments with her, times when he'd been too forward, too pushy. Times when he'd made it clear he wanted sex, when actually he wanted so much more.

He wanted to tell Amanda that it would be all right. But he just didn't know.

Thinking of what she'd likely gone through, what he knew she'd felt judging by the expression on her face during the retelling made him ill.

Josh believed Amanda's father loved her, based on what she'd said. He'd seen many people fight to try to save their loved ones, willingly putting themselves at risk. But her father never should have taken her to visit the injured men in the hospital.

He'd probably thought to teach her a valuable lesson, or perhaps he'd gone strictly out of goodwill, wanting to offer thanks as well as his apologies for what had occurred. But putting Amanda through

such an ordeal, making her deal with the accusations
wrought from grief, had caused her so much harm.

People in mourning, people afraid and worried,
were emotionally fragile, not given to clear thinking.
Of course family members and friends had at first
blamed Amanda—they'd needed a way to vent and
she'd been far too handy.

Her father should have protected her from that, not
exposed her to it.

While standing in the middle of her kitchen, struggling to deal with his turbulent thoughts, Josh heard
the faint tinkle of bells. He paused, lifting his head
and listening. The sound came again, louder with the
whistling of the wind and he went to the window to
look out.

Nothing but blackness could be seen, and a fresh
worry invaded his already overwrought mind.
Amanda was too alone here, too vulnerable. She literally lived in isolation with no one nearby if she
needed help.

Josh searched for a light switch and finally located
one by the sink.

A floodlight illuminated the backyard and an incredible display of wind chimes, large and small,
brass and wood, colorful and dull. With each breeze,
they rang out in soft musical notes.

He also noted the birdhouses and feeders, dozens
of them everywhere, on poles and in the trees.

With his head lowered and his eyes misty, Josh

flipped the light back off and leaned on the sink. Damn, he'd never known a woman like Amanda Barker. She was all starch and hard determination one minute, and so soft and needy the next.

The shower turned off, jarring Josh out of his ruminations. He rushed through the coffee preparations, noting the fact that her coffeemaker only made three cups, proof positive that she never entertained guests.

Rummaging through her refrigerator, he found cheese and lettuce and mayonnaise. He remembered how little she ate and made two sandwiches, one and a half for himself, a half for Amanda. He'd just finished putting pickle slices on a plate and cutting the sandwiches when she appeared.

Josh looked up, and smiled. Amanda's face was still ravaged—her eyes were puffy, her nose pink, her lips swollen and her cheeks blotchy. But the oil and blackening was gone, as was her makeup. She'd tied her hair onto the top of her head, but she'd been hasty with it and long tendrils hung down her nape, around her ears.

Though she was bundled up in a white chenille robe, Josh could see her pale yellow thermal pajamas beneath and the thick white socks on her feet.

Her hands clutched the lapels of the robe and she said, "I told you I wasn't hungry."

Josh lied smoothly, without an ounce of guilt. "But I am, and I hate to eat alone. Even you ought to be able to choke down half a cheese sandwich."

While she stood there hovering just out of his reach, Josh cleared her table. He neatly stacked a small mountain of papers and photographs and transferred them to the washer, the only uncluttered surface available.

Evidence of her continued efforts was everywhere; the papers he'd just moved, contracts, old calendars, fund raising schedules and event planners.

"Can I ask you a few things, Amanda?"

She braced herself as if expecting an inquisition on the fires of hell. "Yes, of course."

Her guilt was so extreme, he knew she wouldn't give it up easily. She'd been living with it for seven years and it was now a part of her. "If you're not interested in getting cozy with a guy, why do you dress so sexy?"

Even without makeup, her big brown eyes looked lovely, soft with long lashes that shadowed her cheeks when she blinked.

"I don't. I wear business suits."

Business suits that in no way looked businesslike. They had nipped waists and above the knee thigh-hugging skirts. And those sexy shoes she wore...

Josh had his own theories, but he wondered if Amanda realized the connection that she'd made.

The night of the fire, by her own account, she'd been caught disheveled, her activities apparent from her rumpled appearance. Now she was always dressed impeccably, polished from her hair to her high heels. With every tidy suit she donned, she made a statement. But she also emphasized that she was a woman.

"Your suits are sexier than a lot of miniskirts." Josh wasn't a psychologist, but it seemed obvious to him. "You also wear stockings and high heels."

She pulled out a chair to sit, and then picked up a pickle slice, avoiding his gaze. "No one knows that I wear stockings."

Josh drew his chair around next to her. "I do."

She glanced at him and away. "You wouldn't have if things hadn't gotten out of hand."

"Okay, let's look at this another way. *You* know what you're wearing. So why do you?"

She chewed and swallowed before answering. Her cheeks colored. "Sometimes," she whispered, measuring her words, "I don't feel much like a woman. I suppose it's my way of...balancing things. For me, not for anyone else."

Josh's heart pounded. She was trusting him, sharing with him. "You make yourself feel more feminine because you're a virgin?"

She shook her head. "No. Because I'm frigid."

He wasn't at all convinced of that, but he'd argue it with her later. "I guess it makes sense. But I gotta tell you, I can't imagine a sexier or more feminine woman than you. With or without experience."

As more color rushed to her face, Amanda stared hard at another pickle slice and then picked it up.

Josh smiled. He had her confused and that was nice

for a change. Maybe he'd eventually get her so con-fused she'd forget her ridiculous guilt.

"What about this house?" he asked. "If your par-ents are rich, why the tiny home? And why a Volks-wagen? I pegged you as more of a Mercedes gal."

She lifted the bread on her half of a sandwich, looked beneath critically, then replaced it. Since she'd only had mayonnaise in her refrigerator, no mustard, he didn't know what she'd expected to find.

"I love this house, so don't go insulting it. I'm just me and I don't need much room. And my car runs great. When other cars won't start in the cold, she al-ways kicks over and gets me where I'm going."

"That's not what I'm asking and you know it."

"I know." She sighed. "Truth is, I live in a small house and drive an economical car because that's all I can afford. I only have what I earn, and it's not that much. But," she added, giving him a look, "I'd have bought this house regardless. I do love it, and now, after being here for a while, I can't imagine living anywhere else."

"What about your family?"

"You mean what about the family coffers?" She shrugged. "My father and I had a major falling out. Since we weren't close emotionally, I couldn't use him financially. I decided to make it on my own."

"What did your father have to say about that?"

"He was naturally furious that I refused his money, doubly so when I took out student loans to finish pay-ing for my college tuition. He didn't think I'd make it, but I've proven him wrong. I have to keep an inexpensive car and house to do it, but I'm totally independent and I like it that way."

Josh watched her bite into her sandwich and waited until she'd swallowed to ask, "What caused the falling out?"

She waved a negligent hand, but her big sad eyes darkened again. "What I did, the fire and the damage—"

His back stiffened, his muscles tightened. "He blamed you?"

"Oh, no, never that. But he's never understood how I feel, either."

"You didn't cause the fire, Amanda."

"No, but I sure caused a lot of the damage. As my mother used to say, a house can be quickly rebuilt, but a damaged reputation is impossible to repair."

Disgust filled him. Josh was thinking rather insulting things about the mother until Amanda clarified, "My mother said that in regard to herself—she'd been seen on camera, in her robe and her curlers."

"She was worried about her appearance in the middle of the house burning down?"

"My mother wouldn't normally be caught dead without her makeup. She was mortified. My whole family was. And it was my fault." Amanda peered up at him. "What she said was true, at least when applied to me."

Josh frowned. "Your reputation is that of a beautiful, giving woman who works hard at helping others."

"To some. To those who don't know it all."

"To anyone with any sense."

Amanda stared over his shoulder. "All of us had our lives, our backgrounds thrown out there to be scrutinized. Everyone knew the girl who'd been screwing around in the woods while a man died trying to rescue her, and they knew my family, my sister who was younger than me, the mother and father who had raised such an irresponsible child."

"Amanda, damn it..."

"That's what the papers called me, 'irresponsible.' All things considered, it's not such a horrible insult." She picked at the crust on her sandwich, pulling it apart. "Things quieted down when I first went away to college. Problem was, though, after about a year and a half, I got another boyfriend. Big mistake, that."

"Every college kid dates, Amanda." He could already guess what had happened, and it made him want to shout.

"I shouldn't have. I should have learned."

"Bullshit. You were getting on with your life. That's what we're supposed to do."

"Sometimes," she agreed without much conviction. "But not that time. I thought I liked this guy a lot. He was popular and fun and outgoing. When he wanted to make love to me, I couldn't. It literally turned my stomach to go beyond kissing."

Josh remembered how she'd clung to him, how hot

and open she had been. He refused to believe that what had happened with a boy in college would hold true with him. She'd been young then, and college boys weren't known for technique or patience.

"I broke things off with him," Amanda explained, "and he got offended. I guess I wounded his male vanity by not getting...aroused by him. He told everyone I was a cold bitch and a tease, and the next thing I knew, someone remembered my name and the whole story was there again."

Hands curled into fists, Josh said, "I gather he spread it around to salve his own ego?"

"Yes. My father was outraged. He wanted me to press charges against him. Sexual harassment, if you can believe that, and slander even though what the guy said was true. I refused, and that's when I took over all my financial obligations."

Josh felt tense enough to explode, but he held it together for Amanda. "Has it been retold since then?"

"No. Well, not until I just told you." She put her sandwich back down and folded her hands on the table. "When I got my job at the mall, right out of college, I met another nice guy. He wasn't like the first. He wasn't overly popular or loud. He was the new manager, shy and studious, eight years older than me. We dated for six months and he was so patient, I really hoped... But I just couldn't."

Talking about it, thinking about her with other men, especially men who had upset her, made him nuts. But there were things he had to know, things he had to ask about if he ever hoped to make headway with her. "Were you sexually attracted to him?"

She looked perplexed by his question. "I liked him."

"It's not the same thing."

"I *wanted* to make love with him."

"Because you wanted him, or because you wanted to prove something to yourself?"

Amanda shoved back her chair so fast it nearly fell over. Josh was on her before she'd taken two steps. He curled his hands around her upper arms and held her still. She was so skittish, forever running from him. "Tell me, honey. Did you want him like you want me?"

"I don't remember. That was two years ago."

"Amanda." He cupped her face and stroked her cheeks with his thumbs. The feel of her soft, warm skin tantalized him. "Don't lie to me, honey."

Her chin lifted. "All right, then no. I didn't want him like I want you. But it doesn't matter."

"I think it does."

"Then you'd be wrong. I can't ever enjoy that part of being a woman. I'm not meant to enjoy it."

*Because she didn't deserve it?* Josh wanted to shake her. "That's idiotic, Amanda, and you know it."

"I tried after that, Josh. I tried a couple of times. But no matter what, it never worked out. I could only go so far and then I'd hate it."

"Hate it how?"

"All of it, in every way. I hated being touched,

looked at. I hated being kissed. It always made me remember..."

He quickly interrupted. "I'm touching you now and you like it. And you didn't mind my kisses at all."

She glared at him and then thumped his chest. "Stop it! You're seeing what you want to see. Odds are if we try this, you'll just be disappointed, too." She thumped him again, then tangled her hand in his shirt and held on tight as she whispered, "Just as I'm always disappointed."

"Like hell." Josh drew her up, kissed her long and hard and held her close. She struggled for just a second or two, and then she clung to him.

Panting, Josh said against her mouth, "Here's what we'll do, Amanda. We'll go really slow. Excruciatingly slow. If at any point you start to feel bad, in any way, you're going to tell me and I swear I'll stop. I won't rush you and never, ever, will I be disappointed. No matter what."

Amanda stared up at him, her gaze filled with hope and excitement—and that damned guilt. Josh had no more doubts. In that single moment of time, he knew he loved her. He also knew he wouldn't tell her yet. She'd get spooked all over again and he didn't want to risk that.

"Can I stay another hour?" he asked, his voice so low and rough he didn't recognize himself.

Amanda nodded and at the same time, asked, "Why?"

"Because I want to kiss you silly." He held her face and put small damp pecks on her chin, her forehead, her ear and the corner of her mouth. He licked her ear and whispered, "I want to lie down in your bed with you and hold you close and feel all of you against me like I did at the park, and I want to kiss you for an hour. And when I leave, I want you to lie awake at least another hour, missing me and wanting me." He looked into her beautiful brown eyes and added, "The way I'll be wanting you and missing you."

Her lips trembled—with nervousness or excitement or fear, he wasn't sure. "It won't do any good..."

"Just kissing. That's all I want."

She ducked her head, smiling, and said, "Liar."

God he loved her. Josh hugged her close and laughed. "Yeah, that was a lie. An *enormous* lie. I want you all the time, right now especially. What I meant is that for tonight, for maybe a week, all we'll do is kiss."

"*A week?* But why?"

"Because I want you to get used to me. I want you to know that you can enjoy the kissing because it won't go any further so there's nothing to be afraid of. I want you to learn to trust me, and to trust yourself again."

"Ah." Her dark eyes shone with blatant doubt. "And when the week's over and nothing has changed? Just how long do you think this super-human patience of yours is going to last?"

"As long as it takes." Josh smiled at her surprise. "Get used to it, Amanda. I'm not going anywhere, so we've got forever."

Amanda's eyes widened and she pushed back from him. Josh wanted to curse. He hadn't meant to say that, hadn't meant to rush her again. Just because he now thought in terms of a lifelong commitment didn't mean the same applied to her. It wasn't that long ago that she had denied even being attracted to him.

But then she drew a deep breath—for courage he thought—and went on tiptoe to put her arms around his neck. She said, "Yes, all right."

"You're willing to try?"

Looking like she faced the gallows, she said, "If you are, then I'd be a fool to say no."

Slightly insulted, Josh asked, "You're willing because you want to test yourself again, or because you actually want me, *me*, not just any guy."

She smiled. "With you around," Amanda told him, "there are no other guys."

Josh picked her up and headed for the bedroom.

# 7

AN HOUR LATER, Amanda felt smothered in a cocoon of sensuality. Her heartbeat raced, her skin tingled, her womb ached and pulled and her breasts...her breasts were so sensitive she couldn't bear it.

But Josh only kissed her.

It was wonderful because she didn't have to worry about freezing up, about not being able to perform. She knew how to kiss, and enjoyed it.

But at the same time, it was frustrating because no matter how excited she got, no matter how much she might want him to touch her a little more, he wouldn't break his word. They'd kiss and that would be all, so she tried to relax and enjoy him.

Relaxing, she found, was out of the question.

"Josh," she gasped, as his lips tugged at her earlobe and his hand opened on her belly. Inside her robe. Stroking.

Normally that would have made her nervous, but not tonight. Not with Josh.

"Yeah baby?"

*Mmmmm.* The way he said that, she no longer objected to the endearment. "When you said kiss—ah!" His tongue licked into her ear, making her tremble

and shattering her thoughts. She stiffened, and he retreated.

"When I said kiss?" Josh trailed damp love bites
down her neck to her shoulder, into the hollow of her
collarbones.

With an effort, Amanda gathered her wits. "I
thought you just meant kiss. You know, on the
mouth."

"I love your mouth," he murmured, then feasted
on her lips for a good three minutes until she felt
nearly mindless again.

He untied the belt to her robe and opened the material wide.

Amanda opened her eyes and watched him curi-
ously.

"I want this out of my way." Josh stared down at
her with heated eyes and a smile of promise. "I adore
your jammies."

Forcing her head up, Amanda surveyed her body.
Her thermal pajamas were warm and soft, a pale yellow trimmed with white daisies on the neck and the
cuffs of her sleeves and pants. Josh hadn't asked her
to strip. No, instead he'd complimented her very silly
sedate nightwear.

It embarrassed her a little, until Josh sat up and
jerked off his T-shirt, throwing it off the foot of the
bed.

"I want to feel your hands on me," he explained.
"Is that okay? You're all right?"

Amanda stared at his hard chest, now smeared a

little with the blackening that hadn't yet rubbed off. His shoulders glistened from the residue of baby oil, and muscles bunched and flexed as he waited for her answer.

"Yes, all right."

Josh groaned. "Touch me anyway you want to, anywhere you want to." He lowered himself back to her, once again taking her mouth.

Amanda knew about kissing, but this wasn't just kissing. This was full body contact, hot breath and a soft tongue and so thrilling she'd never expected it. Every man she'd ever known would have been frantic by now, pushing her for more, trying to convince her with arguments and unwanted touches.

But not Josh. He had large hands and they roamed everywhere, up her arms, over her shoulders, sometimes cupping her face tenderly, sometimes stroking her thighs suggestively. Everything he did was geared toward her pleasure, at her level of comfort.

He seemed to know what she felt before she could understand it. If she stiffened even the tiniest bit, he changed direction. If she gasped in wonder, he intensified his efforts.

She loved it when he touched her belly. He touched it a lot. But he stayed away from any place that might push them beyond the kissing stage, and the result was that she felt on fire.

"Josh, please..."

"Please what? Tell me what you want."

Daringly, she tasted the skin on his neck. He was

salty and hot and she wanted more. "I don't know." She glided her hands over his bare skin, rasping his small nipples, tangling her fingers in his chest hair. He felt so hot, so hard. "I'm afraid to say."

He made a low sound of carnal delight at the feel of her tongue on his neck, her hands exploring his flesh. "Afraid the good feelings will go away?"

"Yes." Guilt nudged at her, memories trying to invade, but above it all was the smell and feel and taste of Josh. She'd probably regret it later, but for now she wanted to be a normal woman, not one filled with fears and reservations. It was what Josh deserved, even if she didn't.

She opened her mouth and sucked on the hot skin of his throat while her fingers pressed into the hard tensed muscles of his shoulders. He tasted *so* good.

Josh dropped his head to rest beside hers on the pillow. "Ah...*damn.*"

"Josh?"

"I think we need to stop," he rasped.

She'd disappointed him! She'd been selfish, taking what she wanted while knowing he wouldn't be satisfied. "I...I'm sorry."

Josh leaned up on one elbow to see her face. His expression was hard and tensed with arousal, his eyes glittering. "For what?"

*For everything.* Amanda bit her lip, then said, "If you want to try..."

"I want more than a quick screw, sweetheart." He

smiled and nipped at her bottom lip, stealing it from her worrying teeth, laughing softly when she gasped.

"I want you," he said, "naked and hot, and I want you laughing and I want you crying. I want you now and tomorrow. None of that has anything to do with having sex right now, but it has everything to do with how you'll feel about me forever."

Her heart stumbled. He'd said it again, used that *"forever"* word twice now, as if they had a future together.

His eyes were smiling and happy, not disappointed. But dark color slashed his cheekbones and she could feel the heat radiating off him, making his skin damp.

He offered her so much; he offered her forever.

Amanda couldn't stop touching him, coasting her hands over his hard muscles and long bones. He was big and macho and very sexy. He was a lot of man, and he claimed to want her forever.

In her heart, she knew forever was impossible. But he was here now, and she was just selfish enough to want a small part of him, for now.

"Will you come over again tomorrow?"

A smile curled his mouth and lit his eyes. "Yeah, I'll be here. But I have a long shift. I work till six. How about I bring dinner?"

"How about I cook dinner?" she countered.

"And after you feed me," he teased, rubbing his palm over her belly, "we can neck some more?"

She touched his jaw where beard shadow rasped her fingertips. "I hope so."

"We'll watch a movie, too. I like the idea of lounging here in your bed, making out and just getting familiar. It sounds real cozy."

Amanda looked up at the ceiling and laughed, a little amazed, a lot confused. "I can't imagine any man saying what you just said. Men want to have sex, not just get cozy."

"Some men, maybe. Not me. Not with you."

Every guy Amanda had ever dated had worked hard toward getting her into bed, and when he accepted that wouldn't happen, he'd walked. Men wanted no part of a dysfunctional woman, a woman who couldn't offer sexual satisfaction. To most guys, that disqualified her as a real woman.

To Amanda, they were right.

Josh apparently disagreed.

"You're making me crazy," she said.

"That's the whole idea." He gave her another hard smooch, then pushed himself off the bed. "I want you crazy enough that you can forget everything but me."

She didn't tell him, but she was already halfway there. And she didn't know if that was good—or bad.

JOSH WAS SO PROUD of Amanda. She stood at a podium and directed people to various tables and displays. Her idea of a charity reception to launch sales of the calendar was brilliant, even if he did feel like an idiot strutting around without a shirt, being ogled by females of all ages.

Amanda had insisted all the guys dress in work gear, sans shirts. Of course, they'd all complied, strutting around with their bunker pants slung low, chests bare, their steel-toed boots clunking on the floor as they moved. But she'd also insisted that Josh carry his ax, which was something Amanda found sexy—not that he understood why.

The fun part was that every time a woman got too close to him, Amanda showed up like a fussy White Knight, ready to defend and protect. Josh chuckled to himself, amused by her, and so damn in love he felt ready to burst.

He was also so sexually frustrated he didn't know how much more he could take. Night after night, he'd gone to see Amanda and every time their intimacy grew, though they'd held to the rule of mere kisses. Still, kissing Amanda was wonderful, because her reactions were wonderful. She literally wallowed in her newfound sexual freedom.

And just yesterday, after nearly a full week of pleasurable torture, he'd held her breast in his hand and felt her nipple pressing into his palm. The moment had been so sweet, and he'd felt so triumphant, he'd nearly come in his pants.

Amanda hadn't objected to his familiarity, and in fact her eyes had gone smoky, her breath choppy, her skin warm. She'd arched into him and given a sexy little moan that drove him nuts.

But Josh had forced himself to go no further. It had nearly killed him, but he'd kept control. More than anything, he wanted her to want him—without restrictions, without any bad memories haunting her. When he finally got inside her, he wanted her to be aware only of the pleasure and the heat and the tantalizing friction as they moved together....

Josh groaned. Much more of that fantasy and he'd be making a spectacle of himself. He stared down at his lap and silently ordered his male parts to behave. He'd been giving that damned order since first starting this strange seduction. His body was about to go into full rebellion.

A swat on the butt, followed by a squeeze, made Josh jump. He turned around, and came face-to-face with Vicki. He hadn't seen her since that day outside Marcos, when he'd told her that his free-wheeling days were over.

"Hey, stud," she teased, then went on tiptoe to give him a kiss. Her mouth was soft and warm, and it moved him not even a tiny bit.

Josh said, "Uh," and looked around to see if Amanda had witnessed the byplay. Luckily, she was busy schmoozing a local society matron who would likely grace her with a sizeable donation.

Watching her, Josh appreciated the pretty picture Amanda made today. She'd worn a trim-fitting peach colored skirt that sported a jaunty little matching jacket and made her skin look velvety. The hem of the skirt landed well above her knees and showed the sexy length of her calves and part of her thighs. Josh knew damn good and well she had a garter and silk stockings on underneath, and knowing it made him sweat.

Pearl studs decorated her delicate ears and a triple-strand pearl collar circled her throat. Her rich hair was swept up with a studded comb.

She looked...edible, Josh decided. Especially since she wore very high, high heels and he could too easily imagine her without the dress, standing there looking delectable in nothing more than her soft skin, nylons, heels and pearls.

Vicki stroked his bare chest, letting her fingertip stroke a nipple. "Yoo-hoo, Josh?"

He jerked around, feeling mauled, like fresh meat. He wanted a shirt, damn it.

He wanted Amanda.

"Sorry." He stepped out of reach. "What did you say?"

Her smile was slow and wicked. "Look at you, all warmed up. I recognize that hot expression in your eyes."

That expression was for Amanda, not that Vicki would ever believe it when she stood so close and was acting so suggestive.

"Glad to see me?" she asked. "Things with Ms. Snooty not working out?"

Josh frowned. "She's not snooty."

"No? She comes across that way."

"She's...timid."

"Yeah, right."

Josh rolled his eyes. "Okay, so she's not timid. What are you doing here, Vicki?"

"I'm giving my fair share, of course. I ordered two dozen of the calendars—one for myself, and the rest for female relatives. They'll be thrilled."

"Thanks." Josh felt like a dolt, but what else could he say?

"Thanks? That's it?"

He sighed. "What do you want, Vicki?" She opened her mouth and with a grin, Josh waggled his finger at her, knowing exactly what she'd say. "Other than me."

Vicki laughed. "You know me too well." She touched his chest again so Josh caught her wrist and held it. He felt exposed enough bare-chested in a room full of people dressed in casual evening wear, without having a woman play with him.

Looking up at him through her lashes, Vicki said, "We had some good times together, didn't we?"

Because he knew women, Josh saw the vulnerability in Vicki's eyes. She needed to be reassured, so he did just that. He kissed her knuckles and said, "We had a terrific time. I always enjoyed your company, hon, you know that."

"But?"

Gently, because he hated to hurt anyone, Josh reiterated, "But it's over. I really am a one-woman man, now. That hasn't changed."

Vicki looked beyond him and winced. "Well, your

one woman looks ready to string you up by your toes. I suppose I should get out of the line of fire."

Josh turned and sure enough, Amanda was fuming. He smiled and gave her a wave, still holding on to Vicki with his other hand, though Vicki did her best to edge away from him. Amanda huffed and turned her back on him.

Finally releasing her, he said to Vicki, "I should mingle."

She just shook her head and gave her farewells. He knew Vicki considered his actions strange, but he couldn't help being flattered every time Amanda showed her jealousy. He was used to women who were openly admiring, women who said what they thought and felt—especially about him.

He had to work hard to get any kind of commitment from Amanda—except when she saw him with another woman.

Mick wandered up next, his suit coat open, his hands shoved in his pants pockets. "Doing a little flaunting tonight, huh?"

Josh made a face. "Amanda's idea. All the guys from the calendar are shirtless, but I swear, some of them are enjoying it more than others."

"Others meaning you?"

"I can think of things I'd rather be doing."

Mick glanced around the crowded room. "Not having any fun here, huh?" It was in his nature to be forever on the lookout. Being cautious was partly his nature, partly his job.

Josh felt like an idiot, but he wouldn't tell Mick that. It wasn't that he was ashamed of his body, but it seemed ridiculous to make such a big deal of it. "I'll survive."

"Since you appear to be the theme of this bash, you better."

Everywhere Josh looked, there hung poster-size pictures of himself as Mr. November. Women would see the pictures, then either seek him out with their eyes and start twittering, or rush to buy the calendar. It was humiliating. "If it'll help make money for the charity, then what do I care?"

Mick looked over the buffet table filled with hors d'oeuvres donated by a local caterer. He chose a cracker piled with pinkish cheese, then eyed it closely. "It's for a great cause," he agreed. "I'd think you'd be enjoying yourself with all this attention."

"Would you?"

Mick snorted. "Okay, this is a little overdoing it. But the thing is, it seems you've given up completely on having fun."

Josh frowned at Mick as he held the cracker eye level and scrutinized it. "Meaning?"

"Meaning you just sent a little 'fun' packing."

Confused for the moment, Josh asked, "Vicki?"

"Yeah, Vicki. I remember her as one of your favorites. Any reason you've decided to become celibate?"

"Ha!" Josh crossed his arms over his bare chest and smirked. "Not in this lifetime."

"Oh?" Mick popped the whole cracker in his mouth and made appreciative noises. "Not bad."

"Just what the hell are you getting at, Mick?" Both Mick and Zack knew he was involved with Amanda. Hell, he'd been with her every available moment. He was here now, dressed in bunker pants and steel-toed boots, toting that damn ax she seemed so fond of, just for her. That should explain it all right there.

Mick searched the table for another cracker. Josh thought about hitting him in the head. "Damn it, Mick..."

"Zack is a little worried about you."

That set him back. "The hell you say!"

"Yeah, seems you've been...distracted." Mick glanced at him, then gave his attention back to the cracker. He sniffed at the cheese and made a face. Glancing around, hoping no one would notice, he set it back on the table.

"Distracted how? And if you pick up another bite to eat," Josh warned, "I'll take the ax handle to you."

Mick grinned and held up his empty hands. "Distracted at work. Zack says it's dangerous for you not to give your full attention to the job. We both figured you were just antsy over things with Amanda, but I gotta admit you have me confused. You two seem tight, but here you are, all jittery. And if you're not tight with Amanda, then why did you turn Vicki away?"

Josh sat the ax against the wall and rubbed his face. "Things are...difficult. Different. That's all. Amanda is..." He shook his head, unwilling to betray Amanda's trust, but wishing he had someone to talk to.

"She's what? Not falling at your feet?"

"Of course she wouldn't do that! She's..."

Mick raised a brow and waited.

"Oh hell, I love her, all right?" The words left his mouth and then he grinned. "I really do. I'm crazy about her."

Mick looked as if that was the last thing he'd expected to hear. It rattled him so much that he picked up the smelly cheese and ate it without thinking, then choked and had to grab for a drink.

Wheezing, he said, "You're in love?"

"Yeah."

"With *Amanda*?"

Eyes narrowed, Josh asked, "Any reason you're saying it like that?"

"No! I mean, she's terrific. Pretty, smart, sexy. It's just that she doesn't..." Mick struggled, then shrugged. "...seem your type."

"She's unique."

Mick downed the rest of his drink in one gulp. "God, that cheese was nasty."

Laughing, Josh said, "That's good old American cheese and Swiss down there on the end, with the fruit."

"Thanks." Mick picked up a plate and moved in that direction. Josh followed. "So, uh, does Amanda feel the same way?"

"What is this, Mick? Are you my Father Confessor? Did Zack send you here to pick my brain and make sure I wasn't screwing up my life? Are you supposed to advise me and set me on the straight and narrow?"

"Yeah, something like that." Mick popped a grape into his mouth and smiled. "Now that's good."

His mood quickly turning black, Josh said, "Just let me go get my ax and then I'll..."

Mick caught his arm, laughing. "Don't bludgeon me. I swear, this was all Zack's idea. He'd have been here himself if Dani hadn't gotten sick. Wynn told him to come, but you know how Zack is, a real mother hen when his little girl isn't well."

"Yeah, I know how he is." Josh knew a buildup of sexual frustration had made him a little less than reasonable. He hoped Amanda told him how she felt soon, because he didn't know if he could take too much more.

"So is it true?" Mick asked. "Have you been distracted at work? And don't growl at me! With all the grief you gave us, you're due for some back."

Josh subsided at the truth of those words. He had harassed Mick and Zack plenty when they were trying to figure out the whole love thing.

Of course, Josh had it figured out. It was Amanda who seemed unsure. But damned if he'd tell Mick that.

"We're concerned," Mick continued. "Rightfully so, too. Hell, even Wynn and Del told me you were acting different. Not that I pay much attention to your moods, but now that I am, I see what they mean. And Zack sees you at work. He said everyone was razzing a probie, sending him outside repeatedly to find a hose winder—which I gather doesn't exist—and you never said a word."

All probationary firefighters caught hell on their first week at the station. As a lieutenant, Josh usually did his best to run interference, but true enough, he'd been distracted all week thinking about Amanda. He'd barely noticed the antics going on during his shift.

"Zack also says you've been slower on the drills."

He'd strangle Zack when next he saw him. "I know those drills by heart."

"Yeah, but that's not the point and you know it. So tell me, what's up?"

"It's private."

Mick gave him an incredulous look. "That never stopped you from butting into my business!"

"I know, but this isn't just my business. It's Amanda's business, too. She has some things to work out, and until she does, we're not...that is, I haven't..."

Aghast, Mick said, "Damn. You *are* celibate."

"It's temporary."

At the look on Josh's face, Mick sputtered and quickly snatched up a napkin. "Oh, this is priceless," he said, shaking his head while continuing to chuckle.

Through his teeth, Josh said, "It's not a big deal, damn it. I know what I'm doing."

"Hey, I'm not the one who thinks sexual variety keeps you young. That's your mantra, not mine."

Josh reached for his own drink. It was that or Mick's throat. "You always were a particular bastard."

"And you never were, not where women are concerned. But now you're hooked and she's making you work for it instead of throwing herself at you." Mick grinned. "This is great. I love it."

"Shut the hell up, will you?" Josh saw nothing amusing in the situation. Of course, if it had been Mick or Zack, he might have seen the humor.

"Damn, you're testy. Okay, okay!" Mick held up his hands when Josh started to reach for him. "Don't start foaming at the mouth. I wanted to get serious for a second, anyway."

His tone made Josh uneasy. "What? More unsolicited advice?"

Mick gave him that dark-eyed look he used to bring criminals low. "I didn't think *you* knew any other kind."

Remembering the hell he'd put Mick through when Mick had fallen in love with Delilah, Josh had to agree. He'd handed out advice—and aggravation—left and right.

"You need to be more careful at work," Mick said. "I know women troubles can rattle any guy, but if there's a fire, you have to be thinking with the right head, and I'm not talking about the one you let make most of your decisions."

Josh bristled. "You saying I can't control myself sexually?" Ha! What a joke. If only Mick knew, he'd be applauding his iron control.

"I'm saying I don't want to see you get hurt."

"I'm damn good at my job." Feeling defensive, Josh squared off and waited for Mick to dare disagree.

Mick didn't give him the satisfaction.

"I'm not questioning that," he said, "just your frame of mind. Being lovesick is all well and good— hell, I personally think you're past due. But don't let your mind wander when your life is at stake, okay? That's all I'm saying."

Josh started to agree, when suddenly he felt a familiar tension. He was so attuned to Amanda, so aware of her on every level, he instinctively felt her presence.

He turned, already knowing she stood behind him.

Hands clasped together and her cheeks pale, Amanda stared up at him. She looked equal parts furious and mortified.

Covering his uneasiness at being caught while discussing her, Josh pulled himself together and reached for her. She felt rigid under his palms, but she didn't fight him when he tugged her to her tiptoes and kissed her lips. "Hey sweetheart. Finally got a break, huh? It's about time. I was feeling sorely neglected."

She said, "Yes of course. You've only got every

woman here following you around, trying to get your attention."

Josh said, "You noticed," and he grinned.

Amanda stared beyond him at Mick, who looked as uncomfortable as a dark, enigmatic undercover cop could look.

Mick drummed up a sad excuse for a casual smile and said, "Hello Amanda. It's nice seeing you again."

"Mr. Dawson. Thanks for coming."

"Mick, please." Mick glanced at Josh, probably looking for assistance though Josh had none to offer. There were still times when he couldn't figure Amanda out at all, when her moods were a total mystery to him.

This was one of those times.

Mick forged on manfully. "Your reception here is a hit. The, uh, crackers are great."

Josh snickered at that and took pity on Mick. "Go mingle. Go buy a calendar. Just go."

"Delilah already bought several. But mingling sounds nice."

"Coward."

Mick saluted him and wandered off.

Turning back to Amanda, Josh said, "It amazes me how such a small woman can make grown men quake in their boots."

She sniffed. "That's utter nonsense, and you know it. You certainly aren't quaking."

Josh lifted his brows. Acrimony? That told him something, like she was pissed. More jealousy, maybe? Somehow, he didn't think so. "Do you have any idea how badly I want to kiss you?"

Her gaze skipped away from his and her shoulders stiffened. "I wanted to talk to you about that."

"About kissing me? You been having the same naughty thoughts as me?"

"I... No! That's not what I meant at all." She frowned, chewed her lower lip, and then said, "I think we should calm things down a little."

Damn, she had overheard. Josh pretended he didn't understand. "Now why would you want to do that? Especially when last night was so nice?"

*Nice*, what an understatement. They'd lain together on Amanda's bed after watching a science-fiction movie and they'd kissed for an hour. Josh, feeling as randy and naughty as a teenager in the back seat of his dad's Chevy, had nonetheless enjoyed holding her close. He'd relished the way she'd gradually relaxed with him, and he'd enjoyed listening to talk about her work and the stupid calendar and her plans for shade-loving flowers in the spring.

Hell, he just loved listening to her—because he loved her.

Amanda shook her head. "I saw you with that woman."

"Vicki?" He squeezed her shoulders, unconsciously caressing her, hoping to ease her just a bit. "She's an old girlfriend. I already explained things to her."

Stepping away from him, Amanda avoided his direct gaze. "Perhaps you were hasty with that," she said.

Josh crowded close to her back, refusing to let her put a physical or emotional distance between them. He'd worked too hard for the headway he'd gained to just give it up. "Mick already has me edgy. Don't piss me off more by suggesting I go to another woman, okay?"

Her head dropped forward as she tidied the table-cloth on the buffet table and sorted the silverware. Whenever Amanda got nervous, her hands got busy. "This isn't right, Josh. None of it is."

He kissed the ultra soft skin beneath her ear. "Mmmm. Feels right to me."

"It's not fair."

"Yeah? To who?"

"To you." She whirled around and flattened both hands on his bare chest. She started to speak, then noticed the attention she drew to them. Plenty of women who'd been watching Josh all along now stared openly. "I'm making a spectacle of us both."

He didn't mind, but apparently, she did. "So let's find someplace to be alone."

"There's no place here. Besides, I can't just sneak off. I'm trying to successfully drum up interest in the calendar. Too many people donated too many things for me to simply..."

"Take time with me?" He knew that shot wasn't fair, but still couldn't stop himself from saying it. "Yeah, that'd be a waste, wouldn't it?"

Her eyes widened. "Josh! That isn't at all what I meant."

He ran a hand through his hair, regretting his hasty words, feeling his frustration rise. But damn it, she was trying to pull away. "I know it. I'm sorry."

"Don't apologize, either. It's just..." She looked around. "You're right. We should talk. Let's go into the office in the back." She lifted her wrist and Josh saw a coiled band with several keys on it. "I can get us in."

The idea of a private talk no longer appealed. Josh had a terrible suspicion that she wanted to dump him. The damn calendar was done, and God knew the thing was a hit. Local groceries, bookstores and gift shops had agreed to sell them. Orders were coming in faster than they could be filled. The hall she'd gotten donated for the night was now crowded with interested parties, and the firemen who'd posed were considered local celebrities.

Amanda had no more use for him.

Josh marched behind her, cautiously holding the damn ax away from other people, feeling more ridiculous by the moment. He'd let her draw him in, let her use him...

The lock on the door clicked open and she stepped inside. Josh pushed in behind her and before she could find a light, he turned her and pressed her against the door.

He'd always been a breast man, and now, with

Amanda's plump breasts pressed to his bare chest, he felt all his repressed lust boil over.

"Josh!"

He kissed her. He kissed her with a week's worth of frustration and with the fear that she'd reject him now. He kissed her the way he'd been wanting to for a long time. He dropped the ax with a clatter and caught her rounded behind with one hand, urging her closer. With the other hand, he sought her breast, squeezing and cuddling, searching for and finding her nipple, wanting to groan when it puckered tight. He stroked her, then caught her straining nipple between his fingertips and plucked, rolled.

Filled with explosive urgency, he ate at her mouth, devouring her.

Until he felt her frantic hands trying to push him away.

# 8

"JOSH PLEASE!" Amanda could barely catch her breath under the impact of that intense kiss and the experienced touch of his hands. She'd been thinking about him all day, stewing each and every time she saw another woman get close to him. She shouldn't care. The whole point of the reception was to share Josh's appeal so more calendars would be purchased.

All the men had shown up shirtless, as she'd directed. One by one, they'd stepped up to the podium with her to be introduced. Amanda had given their names, told what month they could be found, and then they'd removed their outer coats to reveal their hard muscled chests and shoulders. The women had "oohed" and "aahed" as each upper body was bared.

None of them had affected Amanda at all. She'd done her self-assigned job, seeing the men as a means to an end, a way to build up the donation to the burn center, a way to repay her debt.

They were a gorgeous lot, and Amanda was proud of each of them, but she barely noticed them as men.

Until Josh. As she'd suspected, he got the lion's share of attention. When he'd slipped off his jacket, looking chagrined and put out with the whole affair, the women had roared their approval.

All night long, she'd had to watch while the women ogled him and wanted to touch him and competed for his time and attention. His old girlfriend had been especially brazen, but Amanda wasn't surprised. No woman would want to give up on Josh easily, and knowing that, knowing what each woman thought while looking at him, drove Amanda crazy.

*He* drove her crazy.

She'd barely had a chance to talk to him, but now that they were alone, Josh seemed intent on kissing her senseless.

Amanda pressed his shoulders again and suddenly he cursed and pulled away from her, then cursed again when he stumbled into a chair and sent it skidding onto its side.

With shaking hands, Amanda hastily searched the wall for the switch. Bright fluorescent light shone down on Josh's naked back and shoulders, which he had turned toward her. He stood over the fallen chair, the ax on the floor beside it. His tawny head was down, his large hands curled into fists at his sides.

Her chest hurt just looking at him—and then she remembered what she wanted to talk to him about.

Because of her, Josh was no longer being as cautious at work as he should be. He was thinking of her, of being forced into celibacy, when he should have been concentrating on the job. That would never do.

His job was dangerous enough without her adding to it.

She knew what she had to do.

"If you want," Amanda said, her voice sounding hollow in the silent enclosed room, "we can have sex tonight."

Josh snapped his head around. His green eyes blazed with some emotion she didn't recognize. "What the hell did you say?"

Amanda swallowed hard and took a step back. He didn't look particularly pleased by her offer. After the way he'd just been kissing her, after the way he'd kissed her and touched her all week, she'd thought...

"I heard what Mick said," she admitted, hoping he would understand. "I don't want you to get hurt." His narrowed gaze searched hers and she added with a whisper, "If you did, it would kill me."

He took two long strides toward her, then wrapped his long fingers around her upper arms, lifting her. "Why? Why would you care, Amanda?"

Her feet left the floor. She grabbed his biceps, holding on in the awkward position. This wasn't at all what she'd expected. Why couldn't he ever once do as she anticipated? She'd thought...what? That he'd be happy? Anxious?

Her thoughts were in a jumble, but she did her best to explain. "I've hurt enough people. You've been too good, too helpful... Josh, you're a *hero*." Surely he knew that, accepted it. "We need you. Everyone needs you."

For the briefest moment, his hands tightened almost to the point of pain. There was such a look of raw emotion in his green eyes, she flinched away.

Abruptly he set her on her feet and took two steps back. He seemed remote, even angry, when he said, "Why do you want to sleep with me, Amanda? Or should I ask if you *do* want to sleep with me? You made the offer, but then, that doesn't tell me much."

She licked her dry lips and tried to order her thoughts. It wasn't easy with him standing there half-naked, looking so sexy while glaring at her. "We've been fooling around all week."

"Not me." His jaw hardened. "I was dead serious."

"Oh." Her brain seemed a wasteland, not a clear thought to be found. "I mean, with all the kissing and the touching we've been doing, I assumed... In fact, you've told me!" Her head cleared and she crossed her arms defiantly. "You said you wanted to have sex with me!"

"No, I told you I wanted to make love. There's a difference." He shrugged one massive, hard muscled shoulder. "But either way, so what?"

This whole situation got more difficult by the moment. Had he changed his mind about wanting her? Amanda didn't think so, especially given that hot kiss just a minute before. He'd so taken her by surprise, her knees had nearly buckled.

So why had she thought to make the suggestion? Oh yeah, his well-being. "You've been distracted at work," she pointed out, "and not thinking clearly, and Mick seemed to think it's because you're..."

"Not getting any?"

He made it sound so crude. Well, she wouldn't let him bully her or embarrass her. She met his gaze head-on and raised her chin. "Yes."

Josh laughed. He looked at her and then he laughed some more. But it didn't sound like a happy laugh. Just the opposite. "I guess that answers my question, doesn't it? You didn't offer to sleep with me because you want me, not because everything we've done has gotten to you as much as it has to me."

It had, but he didn't give her a chance to explain that. Everything he'd done, every moment with Josh, had been wonderful. Sometimes she couldn't sleep for wanting him. Her need for him increased every day, with every sight of him, every touch, every kiss, until now it was a constant ache. She dreamed of having him inside her, and it was always so good...and then she'd wake up and feel embarrassed and guilty as she remembered that awful night long ago.

But still she wanted him. Her emotions were so conflicted these days, she didn't know what to think or feel. She only knew that Josh was important to her and she couldn't tolerate the thought of anything happening to him.

He bent for the ax, straightened, and looked at her with an expression of emptiness. "I'm not interested in screwing a martyr."

Amanda reeled backward, bumping into the door

then had to move quickly when Josh reached for the handle.

On his way out, he said, "Thanks, but no thanks," and he left the door standing open behind him. His stomping footsteps were drowned out by the noise of the crowd in the outer room.

For a minute, Amanda just stood there, her body and mind thankfully numb so that she barely felt the quaking of her legs, the riotous pounding of her heart, the constriction of her lungs. Her eyes burned with hurt and humiliation.

That *"thanks but no thanks"* had sounded pretty final. But then what had she expected? That he'd wait around forever for her to change? For her to get over her silly phobias and be a real woman? No other man had; no other man would.

She was still standing there, unable to assimilate anything except her sense of loss, when Josh reappeared. He stomped in, cursing under his breath, his face tense.

He took one look at her, groaned and stepped into the room, slamming the door behind him. He propped the ax against the wall and turned the lock.

Amanda stared stupidly at the doorknob.

"Come here." Josh said it gently and reached for her at the same time.

"But..."

"God, I'm sorry." Then he was holding her close to his bare warm chest and rocking her a little and it felt so good, Amanda got angry.

She pushed back and asked with a good dose of suspicion, "What does this mean? Just what are you doing, Josh?"

He smiled and opened his big hand on the small of her back, urging her close again until her belly was against his pelvis and her breasts flattened against his hard abdomen. "Hell if I know," he groaned, and propped his chin on top of her head.

Amanda could feel the solid thumping of his heartbeat vibrating throughout his big body, and the warmth radiating off his skin. She also heard the smile in his tone.

"It's not funny!" Her nose got squashed into his sternum and she inadvertently breathed his scent.

"No," he agreed in a gravelly tone, "it's really not."

"Then why do you sound so amused?"

"Are you kidding?" He kissed the top of her head. "If it was Mick or Zack floundering around like a fish out of water, I'd be laughing my ass off."

Furious and cold one minute, teasing and tender the next. And they said women were fickle. Amanda shook her head and strained away to see him. "I don't understand you."

"I know. Most of the time I don't understand myself." He made that sound like a grave confession. "But damn it, Amanda, I am not going to give up on you."

She frowned. "I didn't ask you to." Then she muttered, "Though I probably should. This whole thing—"

"What *thing?*"

"Us. Me. It's bad enough that you're having to woo me as if I'm a Victorian maiden, instead of a modern mature woman, but..."

Once again annoyed, he asked through his teeth, "But what?"

If he wanted the whole truth, she'd give it to him. "But now, instead of using your...assets to garner more sales for the calendar, I'm warning women away from you."

Josh straightened and his brows shot up. "You are?"

"Yes, I am. Half the women out there are single and, of course, they just have to ask me about you. As if I'm supposed to help set you up or something! If I'd been thinking straight, if I'd been doing what I should be doing, I'd have encouraged them to buy another calendar and get you to sign it, sort of as a way to break the ice."

He crossed his arms over his chest and scrutinized her with great curiosity. "So what'd you do instead?"

Amanda couldn't quite look at him. "I told them you were taken," she murmured.

"Come again?"

Amanda knew good and well that he'd heard her, he just wanted to make her say it again. Well fine. She glared at him and almost shouted, *"I told them you were taken."*

"Ah." Josh flexed his jaw, whether because she'd

irritated him or because he was trying to hide a smile. She wasn't sure. "Why Amanda?"

"Because I didn't want you to get involved with any of them."

"Yet you made me that ridiculous, unemotional offer."

Angry, remorseful and now insulting. She'd about had enough of his mood swings. She reached out and smoothed her hand over his broad chest. Her fingers found a soft curl there in the middle of his pectoral muscles where the hair was thickest. She smiled up at him, and yanked hard.

"Ow, damn it!" Josh lurched, yowled again when she didn't release him, then caught her wrist and held her hand still. "That hurt!"

"Did it ever occur to you," she asked, retaining her hold on his chest hair in a threatening manner, "that I'm not sure how to go about offering? I've never had much practice. Every other guy I've been close to has been the one pressing me, so I never had to offer!"

Now Josh frowned. "I haven't pressed you because I want you to want me. What I don't want is you making some damn offer like a sacrifice. Like you'd be doing me a favor."

*Sacrifice.* So, that's what he thought? And it had insulted his macho pride?

Her eyes narrowed again. "It'd be nice if you explained all this to me instead of being insulting and mean."

Josh softened. He worked her fingers loose and carried her hand up to his neck, safely away from his chest. "I was mean?" he asked apologetically.

"Yes." Amanda put her other arm around his neck and laced her fingers together at his nape. His dark blond hair felt cool and silky on her knuckles. "I didn't know what to think. You're a very confusing, complex man."

Josh chuckled, then squeezed her close. "That's the pot calling the kettle black, sweetheart." She started to object and he kissed her, a softer, gentler kiss this time. "And here I used to think I knew women."

"You do." Boy, did he ever. Josh knew how to look at her, how to touch her just the right way to make her hot and needy. He also had an uncanny ability to read her mind on occasion. It unnerved her.

"Not you," he denied. "You're a mystery, Amanda, always keeping me guessing. I never know what's going through that head of yours."

"I love kissing you," she said. "That's what's going through my head right now."

His eyes darkened, turning a rich forest green. With her gaze snared in his, Josh very slowly brought his hand up over her waist to her ribs, then higher, just below her left breast. Her heart galloped—in anticipation and excitement.

"You liked me touching you, too, didn't you?" he asked.

Breath catching, Amanda murmured, "Yes."

He leaned down, his mouth touched hers, and his hot palm slid up and over her until he held her breast securely. His long fingers were gentle, molding over her, weighing her, caressing. Against her mouth, he said, "I've always loved breasts."

A laugh caught Amanda by surprise, even as she closed her eyes to absorb more of his touch. "As I understand it," she breathed, "most men do."

"Some of us like them more than others." And he growled, "Damn, you have great breasts."

It was the most absurd conversation she ever could have imagined. Josh touched her nipple, rubbing the very sensitive tip, and her voice broke as she said, "Thank you."

"It's not just your incredible rack that turns me on, though."

Amanda couldn't keep up with his verbal nonsense, not while he was deliberately arousing her. She dropped her head onto his chest and groaned.

"No," he said, still enticing her. His fingers closed on her nipple in a soft pinch, and even through her blouse and bra, it was enough to make her muscles brace, her breath catch. "Talking to you, hearing you laugh, smelling you, hell even thinking of you gets me hard."

Her hold on his neck was now a necessity. Without it, she might have slid to the floor in a puddle.

"I want to touch you between your legs, okay?"

Her eyes snapped open and everything inside her clenched and curled against a wave of heat. They were at a reception, hidden away in an empty office with over a hundred people only a few yards away. "Josh..."

"Shhh. Tell me if you like this."

He pressed his hand to her belly, then pushed lower until his fingertips just touched her in a barely there caress. His palm was on her lower belly, his fingers together, not moving. There was only that fleeting press, nothing more. Her wool skirt felt nonexistent. Her body rocked with her heartbeat.

He didn't move any further.

Panting, held in suspense, Amanda rasped, "Josh?"

His mouth touched her temple. "Everything okay?"

His voice was low and rough and added to her urgency. She bobbed her head, anxious to reassure him. "Yes. Fine."

"Good." He kissed her ear. "How about this?"

"Ohmigod." Amanda squeezed her eyes shut as his big hand pushed lower, dipping down between her thighs, stroking, seeking through the layers of material to find just the right spot. She felt hot on the outside, wet on the inside.

"Is that good?"

"*Yes.*" Better than good. Astounding, really.

Other than her aborted attempt at sexual satisfaction the night of the fire, she'd never felt so aroused. And even then, it wasn't the same. She'd been just seventeen, more excited about doing the forbidden and feeling grown-up than about the boy she'd been with.

Those thoughts were morbid and Amanda did her best to block them from her mind. She wanted to concentrate on Josh, not the past. Yet, the past was there, forever a part of her...

"Imagine how it would be," Josh whispered, interrupting her disturbing retrospection, "with nothing between my hand and your body. My fingers are rough from the work I do, but I'd be really careful, Amanda. A woman is so soft here, so tender."

Her body jerked in reaction to those words.

Josh made a sound of pleasure. "I bet you're silky wet right now, aren't you? I'd love to feel my fingers inside you. Or my tongue slipping over you. Or my—"

A fine tension began to build inside her. Her nails sank into his shoulders and she arched against him with a raw groan.

Josh moved against her protectively. He still toyed with her nipple, continued to put warm damp kisses on her face, her ear, her neck while saying such tantalizing, provoking, *stimulating* things to her.

And his hand... Josh's hand was between her legs making her feel incredible things.

"Yeah, that's it," he encouraged, stroking her, pushing her.

A loud rapping rattled the door, making them lurch apart. Amanda barely stifled a small yelp. Josh cursed.

"Josh?" called a familiar, hushed voice. "Are you in there?"

Josh froze, his body taut and hot, his nostrils flared. "I'll kill him."

"Ohmigod," Amanda whispered, then covered her mouth with shaking hands. She was in charge of this project, responsible for its success. And instead of supervising things, she was hidden away, being pawed. Just the way she'd been seven years ago...

She drew up on that awful thought. No, Josh made it all different. He made it all...special, not ugly.

"I swear," Josh muttered, rubbing his hands up and down Amanda's back as if to soothe her, "I'm going to—"

"You have my profuse apologies," Mick said through the door, "but there's at least a dozen people out here looking for Amanda and they'll be checking back here in another two minutes."

*"Damn it."* Josh held her away from him, his gaze searching, concerned. Frustration vibrated through him, shone in his eyes and in the set of his mouth. "Amanda, are you okay?"

*Okay?* She felt weak with mortification and shaky with arousal—and on the verge of discovering something truly wonderful. "Yes."

"Don't look like that, Amanda," he snapped, misinterpreting her expression of wonder. "What we did—"

"Josh, I can hear you," Mick called, "every damn

word. I'll leave if you'll just tell me what to tell everyone else?''

Without looking away from her, Josh shouted,
"Give me a minute!"

Regretfully, Mick said, "That's about all you've got
before the posse is sent out."

With a heated curse, Josh told Amanda, "Don't
move," and turned away to open the door. In a nasty
tone that more than gave away his frustration, as well
as what they'd been doing, if it hadn't already been
painfully apparent, he barked, "What the hell is it?"

Mick answered in a rush. "A whole group of secretaries and assistants from the office complex down
the street just showed up, but all the calendars
Amanda had out are sold. Some women already left
because the calendars were gone, but the secretaries
are a little tougher. They're eyeing the ones other
women have bought and gotten signed, especially if
anyone is holding more than one. You know a bunch
of people bought more than one so they could give
them away as gifts. Anyway, I'm afraid you're about
to have a riot on your hands if you don't get more calendars out here and fast."

Struggling past an amalgam of rioting sensations,
Amanda stepped around Josh and forced herself to
face Mick. "I'll be right there," she assured him. "If
you could let everyone know I'm getting more calendars right now...?"

Mick looked her over, then quickly averted his
eyes. Was it that obvious, Amanda wondered? Could

Mick tell so easily that she'd been fooling around with Josh at the most inappropriate time? That rather than tending to her obligations and pushing sales of the calendar to earn more money for the burn center, she'd been getting groped instead?

*Wonderfully* groped, Amanda corrected herself. Almost groped to the point of oblivion.

Her face flushed.

Evidently, her situation was very obvious, because Mick rubbed a hand over his jaw and stared at the ceiling. "Yeah, sure," he said, sounding ill at ease. "I'll tell them. That ought to buy you a few minutes at least, as long as they know more calendars are on the way."

"Thank you."

"I could, ah, fetch them for you," Mick offered to the ceiling, "if you want to tell me where they're at?"

Amanda wondered if she had a big red G on her forehead for "groped." The way Mick acted, she wouldn't be at all surprised. "Thank you, but I need to get back anyway."

Mick glanced at Josh, and Amanda saw their shared man-to-man look. Mick's expression said, "I tried," and Josh returned a silent "thanks for the effort."

"All right." Mick headed off, saying over his shoulder, "I'll go appease the mob. Just don't be too long."

The second he was gone, Josh closed the door and turned to stare down at Amanda with his fists propped on his lean hips. "Don't you dare start feeling embarrassed," he ordered.

She all but sputtered a laugh. "Josh, *anyone* would be embarrassed right now! Mick knew exactly what we were doing."

"So?" Josh shrugged, the picture of unconcern. "Now he knows we're human. Big deal. He's not exactly a choirboy himself."

Amanda wasn't about to discuss all this with Josh now, not with people waiting for her. Besides, she was embarrassed, but she wasn't exactly ashamed. And not for one single second did she fool herself into thinking *she'd* have called a halt to what they were doing. If it hadn't been for Mick's interruption, they might have ended up being caught in a much more compromising position.

That thought brought another, and Amanda wondered just what position Josh might have initiated. No doubt, he knew dozens of positions appropriate to making love in an empty office.

"What?" Josh asked. A crooked smile tilted one side of his mouth as he leaned closer. His eyes warmed. "What naughty things are you thinking, Ms. Barker?"

Amanda bit her lip, chagrined once again that he could so easily read her. But she was too curious not to ask. "How would we have...you know. In here?"

Josh froze, then groaned and ran his hand through his hair, leaving the dark blond locks on end. "You're killing me." He pretended his knees were weak and slumped against the wall. "That's a loaded question, honey, guaranteed to give a guy a boner. That is, if I didn't already have one, which I do."

Amanda's eyes widened, but she managed not to look. She ended up with a dazed, goggle-eyed stare, but she kept her attention fixed firmly on his face.

Josh laughed and reached for her. "Tell you what. Tonight, when we finish this damn reception, I'll show you."

Her heart lodged in her throat at that promise. "Yes, all right."

Amanda smiled at him, then edged toward the door. If she didn't leave now the damn posse might find her accosting Josh. Seeing him look so disheveled, she paused and reached for her hair with a sudden concern. Would everyone know what she'd been doing? Or was Mick just more intuitive because he knew Josh and his sexual propensities? "Do I look okay?"

Josh touched her cheek with an unsteady hand. "Babe, no woman could look better."

Amanda was still high on that compliment when she slipped from the room and hurried down the back hallway to the rear door. She assumed Josh would present himself out front shortly, and would buy her enough time to restock the calendars.

The frigid wind cut right through her suit jacket and blouse when she stepped into the lot where her car was parked. Silvery light from streetlamps lent an eerie glow to the cold dark night and reflected off the falling sleet, which now covered her car and was turning the lot into a slick treacherous sheet of ice.

The driver's door was frozen shut and Amanda had to work to get it open. She looked around and saw ice hanging heavily from every phone wire and tree branch. The crackling of sleet peppering the pavement mingled with the sound of the howling wind.

It was a miserable night.

Her hands and nose felt numb and her knees were knocking together by the time Amanda headed back in. She wished she'd had enough sense to grab her coat, but she'd been daydreaming about Josh and that carnal promise of his instead. Shivering uncontrollably, arms laden with boxes, she struggled with the heavy back door.

A second later the door flew open and she almost toppled over. *Josh.*

"What the hell are you doing out there alone?" he demanded.

Her uncontrollable shriek of surprise echoed up and down the hallway. Josh relieved her of the cumbersome boxes and Amanda thanked him by punching him in the shoulder. "You scared me half to death," she accused, once she'd caught her breath.

"You need scaring." He caught her arms and hugged her close, sharing some of his warmth. Amanda noticed he was now wearing a shirt and coat.

Through chattering teeth, she said, "I had to get more calendars. You already knew that."

His scowl darkened. "I thought you had them somewhere in the building, not outside. You should have sent me, or let Mick go when he offered."

Her face was still pressed against him. He felt warm and smelled delicious and she said without thinking, "I needed to cool down anyway."

His hands, which had been coasting up and down her back, paused. Then he squeezed her and groaned. "I must be cursed."

Amanda tilted back to see him and got an awful premonition. "Josh, what's wrong?"

"I have to go into work."

Her heart sank. "*Now?*"

"Unfortunately, yeah." He began rubbing her again, in apology, in regret. "One of the supervisors has the flu. He's heading home, so I need to finish out his shift."

Amanda wanted to cry. Her body still buzzed with need, every part of her felt too sensitive, too...ready. She said, "Damn."

Josh smiled. "I know. Believe me, if I had any other choice, I'd grab it."

Her next thought was whether or not he'd come over after he'd finished the shift. She knew she'd gladly wait up. She finally felt ready to take the big step. Tonight could be the night. Sure, she'd had a few ill moments, thinking of that long-ago fire and what had resulted from her irresponsibility, but she still wanted Josh. Fiercely.

As usual, Josh read her mind. "I won't be off till sometime in the morning. Probably around three." Then he cupped her face and tipped it up and kissed her. His tongue moved softly, deeply into her mouth until her shivers were all gone and she felt feverish. "Think about me tonight," he murmured against her mouth, "and tomorrow I swear I'll make the wait worth your while."

With those provocative words, Josh turned and stalked out through the door she'd just entered. Amanda was left with only the churning of lust.

Lust, and something so much more.

# 9

JOSH STARED through the thick, angry black smoke and gave a silent curse. Long before they'd arrived on the scene, they'd smelled the acrid scent and he'd known, he'd just *known*, this particular fire was going to be a bitch.

His muscles hurt, his head pounded and he was so hot it felt like his skin was roasted beneath his turn-out coat. His gear, including the S.C.B.A., or air-pack, seemed to weigh more than the usual fifty pounds, thanks to his exhaustion.

They'd first gone in without hoses, intent only on rescue. They'd accomplished that much while neighbors all shouted at once, pointing, telling them about the shy quiet single lady still inside on the upper floor. The woman, who Josh had carried out himself, was now in the back of the ambulance being tended. She was a skinny little thing, in her late thirties, disoriented, probably suffering some smoke inhalation and shock, but she'd live.

Given the frigid temperatures and general nastiness of the frozen night, it was one of the worst fires Josh had ever encountered.

They worked their asses off with little success.

The fire spread too quickly, feeding off piles of old newspaper and accumulated junk, licking across dry rotted carpet and up the blistered walls. The howling wind seemed to spur it on, rushing in through shattered windows.

Josh's flashlight flickered over a faded floral couch, now turning orange in flames, then over a pile of books, what looked like an antique desk, a rickety footstool. The place was cluttered, proving the small female being treated outside was a pack rat. Josh searched through the house, seeing objects take shape, forming in the dark as he approached them.

He felt his way through the blackness, checking carefully, watching for a hand, the reflection of pale flesh, anything that might prove to be human.

The narrow flashlight beam bounced off a moving object and Josh crawled closer, then heard a cat's warning yowl. Twin green eyes glowered at him from beneath a small round table tucked into a corner. The cat looked panicked, ready to attack.

Josh's thick gloves provided some protection when he snagged the fat animal and hauled it protectively close to his body. The smell of singed fur burned his nostrils and he crooned in sympathy.

His croon turned to yell a second later as sharp claws managed to connect with his flesh. Josh was barely able to maintain his tight hold on the feline.

Three loud blasts of the rig horn penetrated the crackle and hiss of the surrounding fire.

"Let's go," Josh said, and signaled the retreat.

Three blasts of the horn meant the house was compromised. It was get out now, or maybe not get out at all. Everyone began exiting, Josh a little awkwardly given he had a furious cat tucked into his side.

The second he stepped into the snow-covered yard, the fresh cold air hit him like a welcome slap. Josh flipped up his visor and removed his air mask. There were reporters everywhere, mingling with the noisy neighbors. A flashbulb temporarily blinded him and enraged the cat. It lurched out his arms and shot up a nearby tree in a blur of breakneck speed. Perched on an ice-covered branch, out of harm's way, it took to yowling again.

Josh heard his name called and turned. More pictures were taken, but he didn't even have the chance to get annoyed. The woman they'd pulled from her bed hung on the arm of one of the firefighters. She was now wrapped warmly in someone's coat and a blanket, her thin legs shoved into heavy boots to protect her feet from the cold. Her hair stood on end, and she stumbled toward Josh, her eyes wide and unseeing, her face utterly white in the glow of the moon and the reflecting flames.

"My baby!" she screamed, nearly beside herself. "You have to get my baby!" And she lurched toward the house, falling to her knees in the snow, sobbing, trying to crawl.

Josh went rigid. He looked back at the house, glowing red from within. His heart struck his ribs, his muscles clenched. *Goddamnit, no!*

"Please," the woman moaned, "oh please," and she fought against the restraining hands, as vicious in her upset as the poor cat had been.

Josh locked his jaw, trying to think in the two seconds he didn't really have. His senior tailboard firefighter, fists clenched, shoulders hunched, said, "I'll go."

Josh felt sick. This was the type of decision he didn't like to make. "You're volunteering for a blind, left-hand search in a totally involved fire?"

The firefighter nodded grimly. "Damn right."

Josh understood. He'd already decided to go back in himself.

Then, almost like a gentle stroke, he remembered Amanda. Men had thought she was inside, when she wasn't. During the trauma of a fire, it was difficult as hell to be rational, but that was his job, and now Amanda had helped him.

The probability seeped into him, easing past the exhaustion and fear and the rush of adrenaline, beyond his instinct to charge back inside to save a child, regardless of the odds. It helped him to think above the roar of the fire, the consuming heat, the shouting of all the neighbors, the local media and the wailing of the panicked woman.

A *single* woman. Living all *alone*, the neighbors had said. In her late thirties...

Josh took three long strides to the frightened woman, dropped to his knees so he could hold her shoulders. "Where's the baby?" he asked, and got nothing but hysterical sobs in reply.

He caught her thin, ravaged face in his dirty gloved hands and made her meet his probing gaze. "Where," Josh demanded, "is the baby?"

She blinked tear-swollen eyes, sniffed, then covered her face. Her voice quavered and rose as she wailed, "Upstairs. I think he's still upstairs!"

*I think.* Josh drew an unsteady breath, silently praying. "Give me a description."

Wiping her eyes on the edge of the blanket, she nodded. "He's fat, mostly black with a white tip on his tail." She shuddered. "Oh please, please find him for me."

Josh collapsed. All the strength left his body and he slumped onto his ass with a great sigh of relief.

"The cat," he said, and smiled. Without giving it another thought he caught the woman and pulled her into him, hugging her close. "I got your cat, Miss. He's fine, I promise. Look there in the tree." Josh, still supporting her, turned her with his body and pointed. "See him? He's plenty peeved, and howling to raise the moon, but he's not hurt."

With a cry, the woman stumbled away from Josh and ran awkwardly in the too-big boots and long coat. Two men, concerned because she was so frail, raced behind her. Josh laughed out loud, then scrubbed his hands over his face. "Oh, God."

"You okay?" Another firefighter, a friend, put a hand on Josh's shoulder.

"Hell yeah." Josh looked up at the starless sky, felt the prickling of frozen rain on his face, the bite of a cutting wind. "Hell yeah," he said with more energy. "I'm great."

It was another two hours before they'd finished raking the charred insides of the house out to the sidewalk. It all had to be broken apart and hosed down. Normally that was the hardest part for Josh, seeing someone's life reduced to a black heap on the curb. Furniture, clothing, memories, all gone.

But this time what he saw was the woman sitting in the back of the ambulance, dirty and disheveled, wearing someone else's clothes—and cuddling her "baby" wrapped in a thick warm blanket.

Josh was amazed to see her smiling, occasionally singing, and even from where he swung his ax several yards away, he could have sworn he heard that big cat purring in bliss.

Tears stung his eyes, not that Josh gave a damn. If anyone noticed, he'd blame it on the smoke. But in that moment, he made up his mind. When they finished, he wouldn't go home to get some much-needed sleep as he'd intended. He'd go to Amanda, where he belonged. He'd tell her how much he loved her, how much he needed her, and it would have to be enough.

He'd make it be enough—for both of them.

AMANDA JERKED her front door open the minute she heard the rumbling of the approaching car. Josh!

She'd watched the unfolding details of the fire on the news, fretting, sick at heart, wanting and needing to be with him. At first she just hoped he'd come to her when his shift was over. Then she'd decided if he didn't, she would go to him.

Snow and ice crunched beneath her slippers as she ran through the twilight morning to greet him, unmindful of the cold frosting her breath, the wind howling through her robe.

Josh turned off his car lights, and Amanda noticed the sheer exhaustion that seemed to weigh him down as he sat a moment behind the wheel.

Then he saw her.

Quickly stepping out of the car, Josh said, "Hey," and he caught her as she launched herself against him. "What is it, babe?"

He was warm and hard and alive, so big and so strong. Amanda wanted to touch him all over, to absorb him and his strength and his goodness. She needed to know that he was all right, that the fire hadn't touched him.

Her arms locked around his neck and she squeezed him when he hauled her off her feet, out of the snow. She couldn't speak at first, but then he must have decided that was okay. He lifted her into his arms, cradled her to his chest and stalked to her front door with a type of leashed urgency.

Once inside he kicked her front door closed and went straight to the bedroom and the bed, stretching out with her. Amanda just held on, aware of the tension in his muscles, in his mood. He trembled, his face buried in her neck, his breath coming too fast. His thick arms were steel bands, circling her, getting her as close as possible.

Her throat felt tight and she tried to soothe him. "Josh."

Had something happened to him? Just the thought made her frantic, but she kept her tone calm and easy for him. Smoothing her hand through his thick, still damp hair, she said, "Please, tell me you're all right."

He nuzzled into her. "Yeah." His voice was thick with emotion. Rolling to his back and pulling her into his side, he said, "You heard about the fire?"

"It was on the news." They didn't look at each other. Amanda pushed his coat open so she could touch *him*, not leather. He wore an untucked flannel over a soft thermal shirt and he felt warm and hard and—she wanted him naked.

The thought came out of nowhere, but it was true. She wanted to assure herself that he wasn't hurt in any way.

Josh groaned. "I'm sorry. I didn't even think of that."

Amanda went to work on the buttons of his shirt, almost popping them in her haste. "You're not supposed to think of me. Not on the job, not when it's dangerous."

Josh started to protest and she sat up to work his coat off him. He obliged her, twisting his arms free, then giving a raw chuckle when she did the same with his flannel. Amanda tossed them both to the floor. She eyed his thermal shirt, caught the hem and tugged it upward.

"What are you doing, baby?" Josh asked, even as he raised up to help her get it off.

"Undressing you." The second the shirt was free, she saw the red, welted scratches on his neck. Her breath caught. "Oh, God. Are you all right?" She bent closer, touching his hot skin carefully.

Josh smoothed the backs of his knuckles over her cheek. "Yeah, I'm fine. I got that tangling with a fat cat who didn't have the sense to know I was his savior."

Amanda melted. He was the finest man she knew, and right now, he needed her.

She put several gentle kisses on his injured neck and then turned, straddling his legs with her back to him. His boots were lace-up and took her a minute, but she got them free and tossed them into the pile on the floor.

Josh's hands moved up and down her back. While her touch was agitated, his was more so. "When I'm naked," he asked, "will you get naked, too?"

"Yes."

He went still, then suddenly he was as busy as she, yanking at her robe, distracting her from her efforts as he tended his own. Amanda had to leave the bed to remove his jeans. Josh stood to help her. They bumped heads when they both bent at the waist to push the denim down his long muscled legs. Josh kicked free and reached for her, wanting to remove her nightgown.

Amanda didn't give him a chance. She pushed him onto the bed and stretched out over his tall, naked body. She kissed him, holding his face and feasting on his hot mouth, his throat, then down to his smooth shoulders and broad chest. He was alive, unharmed, and for now, he was hers.

The night had been endless and horrifying. She hadn't slept. Instead, she'd sat in bed watching television while waiting for the occasional update on the fire. Knowing Josh was good at his job, that he was well trained, hadn't helped. She just kept remembering how a man had died for her in just such a fire....

The memories had a different effect this time. Rather than filling her with shame that caused her to withdraw emotionally and physically, they spurred her on. They made her want to grab everything she could, every special moment so that not a single second of her life was wasted.

Josh risked himself every day on his job. He never knew when he'd be called upon to fight a fire, never knew which fire might be his last. He was a hero in the truest sense of the word, and he wanted her.

For that, she was very grateful.

Amanda licked at his hot smooth flesh, biting and sucking, hungry for him in a way she had never experienced, not even seven years ago. She wanted to give him pleasure. She wanted him alive with it.

Josh groaned and put his arms out to his sides, making himself a willing sacrifice.

"I was so scared," Amanda said between kisses and touches and deep breaths that filled her with Josh. It still wasn't enough. She didn't know if she'd ever have enough of him.

His abdomen contracted sharply when she put her mouth there, taking a gentle love bite of a sharply defined muscle. He settled one big hand in her hair, caressing, encouraging. "I was, too," he rasped. "I didn't want to go home alone." He paused to groan, then added, "I want to spend the day with you, Amanda."

"Yes." Amanda could smell him, fresh from a recent shower, but still with the lingering scent of smoke clinging to him. She saw traces of soot under his nails, and remembered him telling her how hard it was to remove, even though he wore gloves.

The hair on his chest, narrowing to a silky line down his abdomen, was brown rather than dark blond. But the hair at his groin was darker still, and thick. Amanda looked at him in fascination and awe and barely suppressed excitement.

His erection rose thick and long, a drop of fluid at the head, proving that he was excited, too.

With her heart pounding, Amanda touched him, exploring the hot, velvet-soft skin over tensile steel. She saw him flex with pleasure. Aware of his accelerated breaths, the intent way he watched her, she wrapped her hand around him in a firm hold. Gently, cautiously, she stroked up his length and back.

Josh's body strained from the mattress—and abruptly dropped when she bent and pressed a kiss just above where her fingers held him. It was a light kiss, tentative, but his wild response and guttural groan lured her. She licked up and over the tip, tasting his salty essence.

A sound of pleasure and pain exploded from his chest. His entire big body quivered. While her mouth moved over him, she cupped his testicles in her other hand, cradling him.

"*Damn*," he said, twisting on the sheets, "I like that, sweetheart."

"Me, too." She breathed in the strong musk scent of his sex, feeling swollen with emotion. It was nearly painful, feeling this way about a man.

"Take me into your mouth," he whispered urgently, "as much of me as you can."

Aroused by the carnal command, Amanda parted her lips wide and drew him in. Both his hands settled in her hair, tangling there, pressing her closer.

"*Suck*," he growled, arching his hips at the same time.

Amanda squirmed around for a better position to do as he needed her to. It was wonderful, tasting him like this, making him lose control, knowing he enjoyed her efforts. Long before she was ready to quit, Josh pulled away from her. His movements were clumsy, rough and fast and she found herself on her back on the bed, Josh between her thighs, in a matter of seconds.

He stared down at her, heaving, his face hard and dark and his eyes glittering. Not giving her a chance to speak, he took her mouth in a demanding, tongue-thrusting kiss.

His long fingers were between her legs, petting her, quickly parting her. She could feel her own slippery wetness, heard his low murmur of satisfaction. Her heartbeat thundered in her ears, a riot of emotions clamored for attention.

"I need you *now*," he panted into her mouth. Against her sensitive flesh, she felt the broad head of his penis, and then his penetration, unrelenting, forceful, going deeper and deeper.

She gasped, and he kissed her fiercely again, swallowing the sound of surprise and wonder.

Amanda twisted as he filled her, a little uncomfortable, a lot turned-on. She'd never had a man inside her and she found it to be an amazing thing, given the man was Josh.

He didn't allow her time to absorb the new sensations. No sooner was he all the way inside her than he began thrusting, sliding all the way out and then driving in deep again, harder and faster with each stroke.

With a groan, he pushed to his knees, forced her thighs wider apart and levered himself on one arm. Using his free hand he touched her everywhere, her breasts, her belly, down between her legs where he circled her, feeling himself as he pounded into her, feeling her stretched taut around him, holding him so tightly.

Amanda felt a scream of intense sensation building. She lifted her legs and locked them around Josh's waist—and he was a goner.

He cursed, long and rough and lurid and then he gripped her close, so close she couldn't draw a breath. His face pressed hard into her shoulder and he said, "*Amanda,*" on a broken whisper.

She knew he was coming, could feel the spasms of his erection inside her, the jerking of his taut muscles, the stillness of his thoughts in that suspended moment. His broad back grew damp, heat rising off him in waves. His buttocks were tight, his thighs rigid. It went on and on and Amanda just held him, so pleased, so awed, until he dropped heavily against her, breathing hard, his heartbeat rocking them both.

Long minutes passed and Amanda relished his limp body cradled against her own. Finally, Josh lifted his head. His movements were slow and sluggish. He looked at Amanda, smiled tenderly, then shook his head. "I'm an ass," he said, his eyes twinkling lazily.

Startled, Amanda frowned. "No you're not. You're wonderful."

He smiled again, then stretched and moved to his back with an earthy groan. "Oh, hell." He put his forearm over his eyes. "That didn't go at all as I meant it to."

Amanda touched his sweaty chest. She couldn't *not* touch him.

"I should be horsewhipped," he complained.

"No, you should sleep here with me." She loved the feel of him, the sleek skin, now damp from exertion, over hard planes and hollows. He was so impressive in every way. "Stay all day, and then tonight again. Let me take care of you, Josh. I don't have to go into work and I assume you won't either now."

"I'm off for the next forty-eight hours." He lifted his arm and looked at her with heavy, sated eyes. "C'mere," he murmured, pulling her onto his chest, "let me show you 'wonderful.'"

It was almost six in the morning and they'd both been up all night. Amanda had spent the night worrying and waiting, but Josh had worked hard. She knew he had to be exhausted, going on lost reserve, but instead of sleeping, he kissed her forehead and asked, "Are you okay?"

"I'm astounded," she told him, and rubbed her cheek against his shoulder. "I'm also a little...messy."

"Mmm." Josh stroked his hand down her back, over her bottom, and between her legs. "Messy with me. And with you."

The things he did, the things he said never failed to shock Amanda. She was engorged, her flesh still tingling, and his rough fingertips rasped over her, gently exploring. She caught her breath and he pushed slightly inside her. The careful prod of his finger only served to exacerbate already sensitized nerve endings.

"I didn't use anything," Josh whispered, and began kissing her ear, her neck. He didn't sound apologetic so much as matter-of-fact.

Amanda couldn't assimilate the repercussions, not while his fingers were there, making her crazy.

"I still don't want to use anything," he told her, but rather than explain why, he pushed his middle finger deep inside her, making her gasp and stiffen.

Amanda nodded. She didn't want him to use anything, not if he didn't want to.

Her quick agreement drove him to action. "Spread your thighs wide around me."

She did, and felt him catch her knees to draw them up so she literally sat astride him, but with her cheek still to his chest. It was an awkward position, forcing her behind up.

"Hmm," Josh growled in satisfaction. "Now I can get to you better."

And he did. Feeling open and vulnerable, Amanda curled her fingers on his shoulders and held on. All the tension began building again, quicker this time, making her vision blur, her skin burn. She squeezed her eyes shut.

"Stiffen your arms so I can get to your nipples."

Amanda moaned. She wasn't sure she could move.

"Amanda," he scolded in a rough throaty purr. "Trust me, honey. Raise up. You'll like this."

Swallowing hard, she forced her arms straight.

With heated eyes, Josh surveyed her breasts. "Beautiful. Damn, honey, let me taste you." So saying, he lifted his head and closed his mouth around her nipple to suckle.

A tearing moan escaped her. She was already so aroused, but now his mouth drew at her breast and his finger moved gently in and out of her, easily because her lust and his climax had made her very slick. She trembled. "Josh..."

He seemed to have all the patience in the world now that he'd come. He licked a path to her other nipple and put that breast through the same sensual torment.

Amanda hovered over him, her belly drawing tight, her nipples aching, her vulva hot and pulsing. Josh released her breast with a last leisurely lick and looked up at her. "You're close," he said with a tender smile. "I can feel you contracting. Almost there."

Amanda couldn't answer him. She bit her lip and concentrated on breathing.

"Do you want to come, sweetheart?"

She nodded.

"Tell me how this feels." He pulled his wet fingers from her and found her clitoris, gently stroking.

Amanda tipped back her head, moaning, so close...

Using his free hand, Josh positioned his erection against her and slowly pressed upward. He sank in to the hilt on the first stroke. "Let's sit you up," he said.

Amanda was too mindless with newfound carnality to do anything, so Josh gently guided her. The new position left her filled, impossibly stretched, and it was wonderful.

Josh bent his knees to support her back, cupped her left breast firmly in his hand, and started the rhythm that she knew would make her wild.

"You're so damn beautiful," he whispered, looking at her belly as it pulled tight, at her breasts as they bounced. She flushed, her muscles tensing and she did her best to stifle a scream.

Locking his intent gaze with hers, Josh licked his middle finger, wetting it, then reached down to toy with her turgid clitoris again.

The scream broke free.

Amanda reached back, clutching his thighs for support as her body shook and bowed with her first orgasm. Josh was so high inside her, filling her up, encouraging her, she felt shattered.

It was her turn to drop onto Josh, and she did so just as he cupped her hips, held her to him tightly, and gave into his second release with a rumbling groan.

Their hot sweaty skin felt fused, their heartbeats mingling. In slurred tones, Josh mumbled, "Sleep."

Mindless, Amanda reached out with a limp hand, snagged the corner of the sheet and pulled it up and over their bodies. Just as Josh began to breathe evenly in sleep, she felt him slip from her body. Smiling, she realized she was really messy now, but she didn't care. She closed her eyes on a sigh, and fell asleep.

# 10

JOSH WOKE with a groan and without even thinking, he reached for Amanda. He found an empty bed.

His head fuzzy from lingering exhaustion, he looked toward the bedside clock. It wasn't even noon yet, but it felt like he'd been out cold for two days. His body was lethargic, his brain sated for the first time in weeks.

And he smiled, knowing why he was sated, remembering Amanda's scream as she'd climaxed, how her sexy brown eyes had gone all soft and vague in her pleasure. She'd been a virgin, so snug and warm his brain had almost shut down. She was all his—he'd given her her first climax.

At that thought Josh frowned and jerked upright. His head spun, but he ignored it. *Her first time.* God, he hadn't been gentle and coaxing and understanding. He hadn't eased her into lovemaking.

He hadn't even insured her pleasure that first time.

He'd been a pig, concerned only with his own pleasure. He'd coerced her into giving him a blow job! He'd been wild, like a crazy man, pushing her and...

Naked, Josh threw his legs over the side of the bed and cupped his head in his hands. For weeks he'd been planning to make Amanda limp with pleasure while utilizing iron control over his own urges. She was emotionally fragile where sex was concerned, and more than a little wary about commitment.

He'd hoped to woo her with sex, to show her how beautiful it could be between them. *Ha!* He remembered the way she'd taken him in her mouth, the way he'd instructed her, and he squeezed his eyes shut. What they'd done had been raw and uncontrolled and just remembering made his blood boil.

He pushed to his feet, going over in his mind all the things he'd say to her, how he'd explain and try to make it right.

A quick trip to the bathroom was top of the list. He recalled Amanda saying she was messy, and what had he done? He should have bathed her, cherished her. He should have used his mouth to bring her to orgasm. It was one of the most intimate methods of making love, and it was something he especially enjoyed. But he hadn't tasted Amanda, hadn't shared that with her.

Instead, he'd had her ride him, and he'd been so deep... Josh groaned. At least that second time she'd gotten her own orgasm.

Josh washed up, splashing his face with cold water to clear away the cobwebs. Though he now smelled more like sex than smoke, he still felt coated in soot. God knew he'd scrubbed long enough under the shower before coming to Amanda early that morning. He hadn't wanted any reminders of the fire for fear it would trigger her memories.

Last night he'd needed her more than he'd needed air.

He needed her still.

Josh located his jeans, now neatly folded over the foot of the bed and he stepped into them. He didn't bother with the zipper or the snap and despite the chill of the air, he never gave his shirt a second thought. The moment he entered the small living room, his eyes were drawn to her.

She sat at the tiny kitchen table, the morning paper open before her and a blank, almost shocked look on her face.

*Damn, damn, damn.* Josh strode to Amanda and pulled her from the chair. He'd tell her he loved her and she'd just have to accept it. Sex was great, damn it, not something to shy away from, not something to mentally link to a bad memory. Sex between them was so incredible he didn't know how he'd survived.

So what that he'd shown her the more carnal side to sex, rather than the gentle beauty of it? He was a man, and he didn't see a thing wrong with enjoying a woman's body in every way possible.

Those thoughts had him shaking.

"Amanda..." he started, but she looked at him and there were tears in her big brown eyes that stopped his heart. She glanced away at the paper, opened to an article about the fire. Accompanying the text was a large color picture of him, carrying that ungrateful cat. He was backlit by the fire, and the photo looked more staged than anything.

Josh released her to pinch the bridge of his nose. His head pounded. "Sweetheart..."

With shaking fingers, Amanda touched his mouth. "I have to tell you something."

He felt sick. "Me first." He drew a bracing breath. "I love you."

Her eyes opened wide in shock. Her mouth moved, but nothing came out.

"I love you, damn it!"

She blinked at his raised voice and stepped away from him. Even rumpled from a night of debauchery, wearing only a robe, Amanda managed to look elegant. Her hair had been brushed and her nails were pink and he wanted her again. Right now. He eyed the cluttered kitchen table. Probably not sturdy enough, he decided. He shook his head.

"Amanda," he warned, about ready to lose his cool, "you better say something and fast."

She nodded, and gestured at the paper without looking at it. "I saw that and realized I should use it to help promote the calendar. You're a remarkable hero and the whole town knows it by now. It's...great publicity."

Josh locked his thighs. The hell she would. The hell he'd let her! Last night had been—

"But I knew I couldn't."

His anger died a rapid death.

She turned her face up to him, appearing dazed

again. "I don't want to share you anymore. That damn reception was hard enough, having all those women fawn over you and knowing what they were thinking because I was thinking it, too."

His tension eased. Cautiously he asked, "What were you thinking?"

"How much I wanted you. How sexy you are, how heroic and wonderful and—"

"I'm just me, babe." And he reiterated, "And I love you."

She swallowed. "I need to start getting things set up for the next calendar."

"The *next* calendar." Her verbal leaps made his head spin. Two more seconds and he was carrying her back to bed for more of that primal mating that made *him* feel a whole hell of a lot better.

"I'd like to make it a yearly event. All kinds of possibilities occurred to me, only..." Amanda bit her lip, then forged on. "Only I can't stand the thought of sharing you."

Josh smiled and explained, "You don't have to share me."

She put a hand to her forehead and looked away. "I don't own you."

"Marry me." He made the offer with a racing heart and a lot of uncertainty. "That's close enough isn't it?"

Amanda whipped around to face him, dropped into her seat, and watched him with the same fascination she might have given a snake. "You want to marry me?"

Josh went to his knees in front of her. He really had to make her understand. "I've known a lot of women—"

She put her hands over her ears, and he pulled them away. Amanda was such a jealous little thing—and he loved it.

"I've had a lot of fun, Amanda," he explained. "But no one has ever made me feel like you do." He carried her hand to his chest, held it there over his heart. "I *love* you. I want to make babies with you and plant gardens and go on family vacations and all that." Josh frowned with sincerity. "I want us to grow old together. And I damn well want you to tell me you love me, too."

She started to speak, but he wasn't ready for her to yet. He had a few more points to make. "Amanda, you do love me, you know. Last night you were incredible. I'm sorry I lost my head there, but you're just too much—"

"I'm just me!"

"—and once you touched me, well, baby I went a little nuts." Josh shrugged. "There's nothing wrong with us having great sex. I'd meant to be really gentle and romantic, but it didn't work out that way. I'd been thinking about you all night and I guess I was half-cocked before I got here."

Amanda choked at his wording, and then sputtered, "I told you, you shouldn't think about me when you're working!"

"You," Josh told her, "are never far from my mind." He pulled her from the chair and into his lap on the floor. Any space between them was too damn much. "Besides, thinking about you is what saved the day."

Josh explained about the cat and how her experience made him stop and think. "If it hadn't been for loving you, I'd have followed my gut instinct and gone back in that house last night, looking for an infant. Then who knows what might have happened to me."

"No!" Amanda curled around him, desperate and sweet, protective even though he outweighed her by over a hundred pounds.

Cradling her head to his chest, Josh said, "What happened to you was awful, sweetheart, but it's in the past and I'm here now. *I love you.*"

"I love you, too."

Josh froze. He grabbed her shoulders and tried to lever her away so he could see her face, but she clung like a stubborn vine. "Amanda!"

He felt her smile against his throat. "That's what I was going to tell you. Last night, you needed me. Not just a body, not just any woman. You came to me and I knew you needed *me.*"

"Hell, yes I need you! Isn't that what I've been saying?"

"You didn't have to work at getting me into bed because I'd already decided I wanted you there. Everything was different because you're different and how I feel about you is different."

His chest expanded, with love and a dozen other elusive emotions. "You love me?"

"Yes. So how can making love with you be anything but wonderful?"

Josh squeezed her until she squeaked. "You little sneak! I've been in agony here, trying to figure you out, trying to decide how to get you to say 'I do,' and all along you knew you loved me."

"You wouldn't let me tell you."

"You only wanted to talk about another damn calendar."

Now she pushed back to see him, and she grinned. "I will."

He frowned suspiciously. "You will what?"

"I will marry you."

"Oh." Josh wanted to shout, to jump up on the table and dance, to drag Amanda to the bedroom and strip her naked. He just nodded. "Good. What a relief."

"And I will do another calendar—"

He groaned and started to topple to the floor.

Amanda laughed and pulled him upright "—but you won't be in it."

"Thank God."

"I want new blood," she said, making him scowl with his own share of budding jealousy. "This is turning out even bigger than I'd first planned. The amount of money we made last night was astronomical. I have all kinds of ideas for letting women in on choosing the models for next year. This time we'll include the paramedics, and maybe we'll even be able to talk Mick into..."

Josh pulled Amanda down to the floor as he reclined, arranging her on top of him.

"Josh! What are you doing."

"I want you to make love to me again."

"Oh." She relaxed.

"And I want you to quit talking about other men. I don't like it."

"I am doing the calendar." She levered herself up, digging her pointy elbows into his chest to scowl at him, just in case he didn't hear the seriousness in her tone. "I'm good at it and I enjoy doing my share to help."

Josh slanted her a look. "You aren't doing it for retribution? This isn't your idea of donning a hair shirt?"

"I'll always feel horrible over what happened that night, Josh. There's no way that'll ever change."

"I'll always love you," Josh whispered. "There's no way that will ever change."

Amanda smiled, bent and kissed him sweetly. "No," she said, "I'm not mentally flogging myself. Not anymore. I just want to help a worthy cause. I've seen now how much the money helps."

"Okay. I'll help too—just not by posing ever

again." Josh caressed her behind. "Can we live here?"

Amanda had just started to stretch out over him again, but drew herself back up. "What?"

"After we're married," he explained. "I'm thinking we could do a large addition, something that would work well with the existing structure and the grounds. We'll need room for babies and all my stuff, a bigger kitchen and another bathroom."

Amanda laid down on him and hugged him tight. "Yes, I'd love that. Living here with you would be perfect."

He held her hips against his growing erection. "You wanna have a baby right away?"

She laughed, leaned up to look at him, then laughed some more. Her body shook atop his and Josh had to smile. Her laughter was such a turn-on, he started inching up the hem of her robe to get to her luscious behind.

"My parents won't believe this."

"Hmmm?"

"That after everything, I've fallen crazy nuts in love...with a firefighter."

# _____Epilogue_____

"MICK, _YOU HAVE TO_ move your hand so I know which guy to vote for."

"I'll cast the vote for you. Hand me your card."

Amanda laughed as she watched Mick and Zack doing their best to keep their wives from viewing the strutting men on stage. They'd paid big money in the name of charity to get front row tables for the event, but now they were turning into prudes. Amanda had every faith that Del and Wynn could hold their own.

Josh was backstage with the men, directing them on when to showcase their assets, while constantly heckling and provoking the young men. He enjoyed his role as assistant and supervisor much more than being a model.

Amanda couldn't imagine being happier. She was now the president of the Firefighter's Calendar yearly production, and as he'd promised, Josh freely gave his help. He was, as she'd accepted from the first, a most remarkable man. And he was all hers.

They'd married two months ago. Their wedding was a huge elaborate celebration and Wynn and Del had teased her mercilessly about her fancy lace and pearl dress, her long train, her veil. But when they'd appeared in their own lacy, feminine gowns, as part of the procession, Mick and Zack had nearly fallen over. Their eyes had glazed and their shoulders tensed and Josh laughed out loud at them.

Amanda learned that the men didn't see their wives dressed up very often, and apparently, seeing them thus was a huge turn-on. She'd heard Wynn whisper to Del that dressing up more often might not be such a bad idea. They'd both turned to Amanda, and said she'd have to give them some tips. Amanda really liked them both and valued their friendship.

Her parents had attended the wedding, along with her sister, and of course, they all loved Josh. He charmed them easily, all the while holding Amanda close.

To Amanda's surprise her father had gotten teary eyed when he hugged her. They'd had regular, friendlier contact since.

Josh stepped up behind Amanda and put his large hot hands on her belly. "You feeling okay?"

She leaned her head back on his shoulder. "I feel fabulous."

"No sickness?"

Amanda laughed. "Josh, I just found out I'm pregnant two days ago!"

He kissed her temple. "I'm going to take such good care of you."

"Mmmm."

"Mick tells me pregnant ladies are always horny."

Amanda sputtered a laugh. Del was in the family

way too, but then, Amanda doubted that had anything to do with her heightened sexuality. As far as she'd been able to tell, both Wynn and Del were always willing to indulge in a little physical love-play with their husbands.

Now that she'd been with Josh, Amanda totally understood that sentiment. All he had to do was look at her and her knees went weak. She felt weak now, and they were in the middle of a special program!

With that thought, Amanda gave her attention back to the stage.

"If I'd have put you up there," Amanda said, eyeing the young firefighter now flexing his muscles and grinning at the feminine catcalls, "we'd have made a fortune."

"You'll make a fortune anyway and you know it. Besides, my wife is territorial. She hates having me ogled by other women, and I love her too much to upset her."

Amanda turned into his arms and hugged him fiercely. The past, for her, was just that. In the past. All the hurt, all the guilt, were now faded memories, buried beneath the incredible love she shared with an incredible man.

He was a hero. He was *her* hero. And working together on the calendar benefit, they'd make a big difference to a lot of people. She couldn't ask for anything more.

# CALL THE ONES YOU LOVE OVER THE HOLIDAYS!

**Save $25 off future book purchases when you buy any four Harlequin® or Silhouette® books in October, November and December 2001,**

### *PLUS*

**receive a phone card good for 15 minutes of long-distance calls to anyone you want in North America!**

## WHAT AN INCREDIBLE DEAL!

Just fill out this form and attach 4 proofs of purchase (cash register receipts) from October, November and December 2001 books, and Harlequin Books will send you a coupon booklet worth a total savings of $25 off future purchases of Harlequin® and Silhouette® books, AND a 15-minute phone card to call the ones you love, anywhere in North America.

Please send this form, along with your cash register receipts as proofs of purchase, to:

**In the USA:** Harlequin Books, P.O. Box 9057, Buffalo, NY 14269-9057
**In Canada:** Harlequin Books, P.O. Box 622, Fort Erie, Ontario L2A 5X3
Cash register receipts must be dated no later than December 31, 2001.
Limit of 1 coupon booklet and phone card per household.
Please allow 4-6 weeks for delivery.

---

**I accept your offer! Enclosed are 4 proofs of purchase. Please send me my coupon booklet and a 15-minute phone card:**

Name: _____

Address: _____ City: _____

State/Prov.: _____ Zip/Postal Code: _____

Account Number (if available): _____

---

**097 KJB DAGL**
PHQ4013

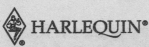

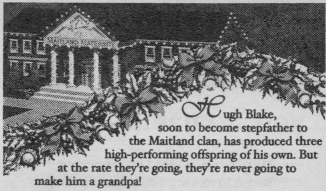

*H*ugh Blake,
soon to become stepfather to
the Maitland clan, has produced three
high-performing offspring of his own. But
at the rate they're going, they're never going to
make him a grandpa!

There's *Suzanne*, a work-obsessed CEO whose Christmas spirit
could use a little topping up....

And *Thomas*, a lawyer whose ability to hold on to the woman
he loves is evaporating by the minute....

And *Diane*, a teacher so dedicated to her teenage students she
hasn't noticed she's put her own life on hold.

But there's a Christmas wake-up call in store
for the Blake siblings. Love *and* Christmas miracles
are in store for all three!

## *Maitland Maternity Christmas*

A collection from three of Harlequin's favorite authors

# Muriel Jensen
# Judy Christenberry
# &Tina Leonard

Look for it in November 2001.

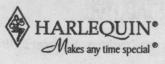